Anonymous

A Souvenir Guide to Boston and Environs

Anonymous

A Souvenir Guide to Boston and Environs

ISBN/EAN: 9783337191320

Printed in Europe, USA, Canada, Australia, Japan

Cover: Foto ©Andreas Hilbeck / pixelio.de

More available books at **www.hansebooks.com**

A SOUVENIR GUIDE TO BOSTON

AND ENVIRONS

G. W. ARMSTRONG
PUBLISHER ~ BOSTON

THIS IS

E. G., DAVIS

The Confectioner,

OF

83 MAIN STREET,

BOSTON,

C. D.

Who makes Wedding Cake, Ice Cream, Sherbets, and Fancy Ices. . . ○ ●

WHOLESALE AND RETAIL.

Families, Lodges, Churches, Picnics, and Private Parties supplied at short notice.

TELEPHONE 258—2.

Otis E. Weld & Co.

Successors to JOHN D. & M. WILLIAMS,

. . . IMPORTERS OF . . .

Wines and Spirits

. . . AGENTS . . .

Louis Roederer Champagne

185 and 187 State Street,
BOSTON, MASS.

THE SEASHORE, LAKE, AND MOUNTAIN
HEALTH AND PLEASURE RESORTS

OF

Eastern and Northern New England

Are easily accessible by the frequent trains of the

BOSTON & MAINE
. . . . RAILROAD . . . .

If you desire to visit some of the *historic* towns within easy reach of Boston, a short journey will take you to *Salem. Mass.; Marblehead, Mass.; Concord, Mass.; Lexington, Mass.; Newburyport, Mass.; and Portsmouth, N. H.*

ELEGANTLY EQUIPPED FAST TRAINS,

With Parlor and Sleeping Cars, to the Coast points: *York Beach, Kennebunk, Old Orchard Beach, Bar Harbor, St. Andrews, and St. John.*

To the White Mountains,
Green Mountains,
Adirondack Mountains.

THE LAKE REGIONS OF

Maine, New Hampshire, and Vermont.

Summer Excursion book, giving complete list of tours, routes, and rates, hotel and boarding-house list, maps, etc., may be obtained free at any principal office of the company, or will be mailed by Passenger Department, B. & M. R. R., Boston.

Boston City Ticket Office, 214-218 Washington Street, corner of State Street.

D. J. FLANDERS,
General Passenger and Ticket Agent.

AFTER SEEING BOSTON......

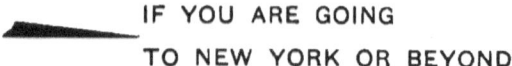

IF YOU ARE GOING

TO NEW YORK OR BEYOND

Choose one of the Excellent Routes Operated by the

New York & New England Railroad

The "AIR LINE LIMITED" EXPRESS TRAIN, Pullman Vestibuled from end to end, luxuriously equipped with Buffet Smokers, Parlor Cars, Coaches, and Dining Car between Boston and Willimantic, leaves either city 3.00 p.m. every day in the year; due opposite city 9.00 p.m.

...Norwich Line...

INSIDE ROUTE.

New Vestibuled Steamboat Express Train with Parlor Cars attached leaves Boston 7.15 p.m., week days, connecting at New London with one of the fine steamers "City of Lowell" (new) or "City of Worcester." Due New York, Pier 40, North River, 7.00 a.m.; connecting with through trains for South and West.

PROMENADE CONCERTS ON STEAMERS EVERY EVENING.

STATEROOMS $1.00, $1.50, AND $2.00 EACH. BERTHS FREE.

Finest Cuisine and Service. Meals served a la carte or table d'hote dinner 75 cents.

TICKET OFFICES { 322 Washington Street.   Telephone 1,244 { *BOSTON.*
{ Station foot Summer Street.   Telephone 3,989 {

GEO. F. RANDOLPH,   **W. R. BABCOCK,**
General Traffic Manager.   *General Passenger Agent.*

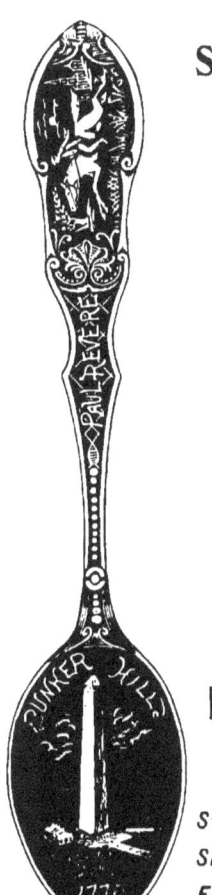

BUNKER HILL MONUMENT — Monument Square, Charlestown District.

A SOUVENIR GUIDE

TO

BOSTON

AND

ENVIRONS.

WITH MAPS AND ILLUSTRATIONS.

BOSTON.

G. W. ARMSTRONG, PUBLISHER.

TABLE OF CONTENTS.

(3)

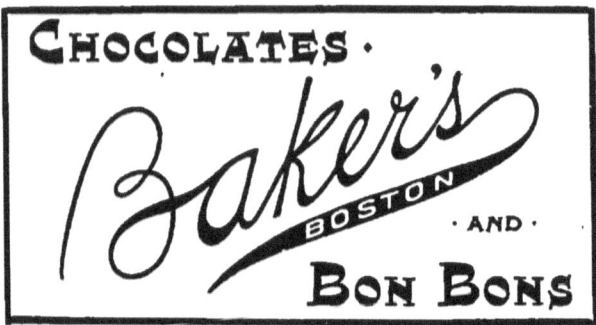

LIST OF ILLUSTRATIONS.

(5)

G. W. Simmons & Co., Oak Hall, Boston, 32 to 44 North Street, are the Oldest Established Clothiers in Boston. They deal in everything worn by men, youths, and boys.

They are New England's headquarters for military goods of every kind. Also, for uniform and livery work, flags, banners, and laces. If you want good work you may be sure of it at G. W. Simmons & Co.'s, Oak Hall, Boston, 32 to 44 North St.

I.

AN INTRODUCTION TO BOSTON.

Boston, the beautiful Puritan city, has many gateways through which the pilgrims, upon whatever errand bent, may enter her goodly precincts. And she has much to offer, to all who will come to her, in the way of historic relics, treasures of literature and art, and facilities for study or business. Her older streets may be winding and narrow, but they are picturesque and full of suggestions of that past in which all Americans have an interest, and of which they have a right to be proud. Many of these quaint old thoroughfares lead to shrines which, as long as they exist, will attract tourists and will help to keep alive feelings of patriotism and loyalty. There is no city in the world where the spirit of hospitality is more boundless, or where all that pertains to the comfort of the guest is more accessible.

A feeling of uncertainty and dread is apt to possess the mind of one who is entering a strange city, and the friendly words of direction and caution given in this chapter are intended to remove, as far as may be possible, the embarrassment and discomfort which are natural to inexperienced travelers. There are six railway stations in Boston and many landing places for passengers from trans-Atlantic and coastwise steamers. In the following pages each of these points of arrival is noted, and suggestions are given in regard to transportation of baggage, hotels, and other matters of interest to those who would become acquainted with Boston.

Railway Stations.

The Boston & Albany Railroad has its depot on Kneeland Street, between Utica and Lincoln streets. This is the point of departure for through trains for the West, via the New York Central & Hudson River Railroad.

The Boston & Maine Railroad System occupies the new Union Station on Causeway Street, between Nashua and Haverhill streets.

This system, in addition to its main line, comprises the Boston & Lowell division, the Eastern division, and the Central Massachusetts division.

The Fitchburg Railroad—Hoosac Tunnel Route—also occupies the new Union Station on Causeway Street, between Nashua and Haverhill streets.

The New York & New England Railroad Station is on Atlantic Avenue, foot of Summer Street. In connection with this railroad is the Norwich Line of Sound steamers for New York. From this depot the celebrated white train leaves daily, at 3 P. M., for New York. This is a favorite train with experienced travelers. The main line of this road terminates at Newburgh, N. Y., on the Hudson.

The New York, New Haven & Hartford Railroad—*"Old Colony" System*—occupies the " Old Colony" Depot, corner of Kneeland and South streets, from which the trains of all the branches of this system, except the " Providence division," leave. Trains for Cape Cod, Martha's Vineyard, and many other seaside resorts start from this station.

Old Colony System — Providence Division — has its depot in Park Square, on Columbus Avenue, opposite Elliot Street. Operated in connection with this division of the Old Colony line are the Fall River, Providence, and Stonington lines of Sound steamers.

Remarks on the Various Railway Stations.

Much of the traveler's comfort depends upon the railway stations with which he has to do in making a journey. Those of Boston will compare favorably with the stations of other great cities of the United States. The waiting-rooms are spacious and comfortably furnished; the toilet-rooms and barber shops are neat and orderly, and the attendants are obliging and civil when giving information. In each one of the stations will be found lunch rooms or counters, as well as restaurants, where well-cooked meals, at reasonable prices, may be had at any hour of the day.

Telegraph and telephone offices, news-stands, flower and fruit stands, and information bureaus are also located in all of the stations.

Ladies arriving alone in Boston will always find a matron in charge of the waiting-room who will answer questions and give information and suggestions which it will be quite safe to follow.

MAIN ENTRANCE, UNION STATION.

The Finest 10c Cigar

. . IS THE . .

Key West
Rosa

SOLD AT ALL STATIONS ON THE

 Boston & Albany,
Boston & Maine, and
Fitchburg Railroads,

. . . BY . . .

GEO. W. ARMSTRONG.

. . People passing through Boston who have to wait over for an hour or two for a train can board a street car at the entrance of any of the stations and take a ride which will not only refresh them, but which will give them a comprehensive glimpse of Boston.

From *Park Square Station* it is but a minute's walk to the beautiful Public Garden, and here the tired traveler may wander among the flowers, rest under the shadow of the fine old trees, or go boating on the lake. If there is time enough for the traveler to pass from the garden and cross Charles Street to the Common and stroll about its shady walks and malls, he will carry away a mental picture which, for beauty, interest, and restfulness, can not be rivaled.

The new *Union Station*, with a frontage of 367 feet on Causeway Street, presents some features which are worthy of note. It is one of the largest railway stations in the world, and 100,000 people daily pass through its portals. The grand entrance is under the largest arch, but one, in the country. The main waiting-room will seat several hundred people, and the marble toilet-rooms and special waiting-rooms will all meet with the approval of those who know the annoyances as well as the pleasures of travel. From either of the ten local ticket windows tickets to 686 different points may be purchased, while from the five other windows tickets may be bought to any railway station in the United States, Canada, or Mexico. The hackstand at this station is 100 feet square, and is under the station roof, a fact which will be appreciated by travelers in stormy weather.

From the front of this station cars may be taken to any part of the city or suburbs, and those who have to wait for a train may find rest and recreation in this way. It may interest the traveler to know that over 600 trains leave this station every day, and that night is turned into day by 300 arc and over 5,000 incandescent electric lights.

Sound Steamers for New York.

People journeying between Boston and New York will often find it pleasant and convenient to patronize one of the lines of Sound steamers. The advantages which these boats offer, especially in warm weather, are freedom from the heat and dust of the railway, and a clean, luxurious stateroom.

The boats of the *Fall River* and *Providence* and *Norwich* lines are floating palaces, wherein one may enjoy all the comforts of a

2

first-class hotel and reach his destination in the morning ready for a day of business or pleasure. (See *New York & New England Railway* and *Old Colony Railroad.*)

Fall River Line.— Park Square Station.
Norwich Line.— New York & New England Railroad Station, Atlantic Avenue, foot of Summer Street.
Providence Line.— Park Square Station.
Stonington Line.— Park Square Station.

Steamship Landings.

Trans-Atlantic Steamships.—

Anchor Line.— (London). Commonwealth Dock, South Boston. Agents, Henderson Brothers, 7 and 9 State Street.
Allan Line.— (Glasgow). No. 6 Hoosac Tunnel Dock, Charlestown. Offices, 80 State Street.
Cunard Line.— (Liverpool). Cunard Docks, foot of Clide Street, East Boston. Office, 99 State Street.
Warren Line.— (Liverpool). Hoosac Tunnel Dock, Charlestown. Warren & Co., agents, 125 Milk Street.
Leyland Line.— (Liverpool). Grand Junction Dock, East Boston. Agents, W. H. Lincoln & Co., 14 State Street.
Furnace Line.— (London). Hoosac Tunnel Dock, Charlestown. Furnace, Witlely & Co., 85 Water Street.
Johnston Line.— (London and Hamburg). N. Y. & N. E. Dock, South Boston. W. J. Johnston & Co., Chamber of Commerce.
Wilson Line.— (Hull). N. Y. & N. E. Dock, South Boston. Agent, 88 Kilby Street.

Coastwise and River Steamers.—

Boston & Bangor Steamship Company.— Foster's Wharf. William H. Hill, general manager. (Bangor and intermediate points on Penobscot River.)
Kennebec Steamboat Company.— Lincoln's Wharf. Charles H. Hyde, agent. (Bath, Richmond, Gardiner, Hallowell, and Augusta.)
Yarmouth Steamship Company.— Lewis Wharf. Office, 64 Chatham Street. (Yarmouth, N. S., and St. John, N. B.)
International Steamship Company.— Commercial Wharf. (Digby and Annapolis, N. S.; Eastport, Maine; St. John, N. B., and Halifax, N. S.)
Boston & Gloucester Steamship Company.— Central Wharf. E. S. Merchant, agent, 244 Atlantic Avenue.
Canada Atlantic Steamship Company.— Lewis Wharf. R. B. Gardner, manager. (Halifax.)
For Philadelphia.— Central Wharf. E. B. Sampson, agent, 70 Long Wharf.
For Baltimore and Norfolk.— Battery Wharf. George E. Smalley, agent.
For Savannah.— Lewis Wharf. Richardson & Barnard, agents.

PARK SQUARE STATION—Columbus Avenue and Providence Street.

TALK ABOUT GOOD CIGARS!
DID YOU EVER SMOKE A
QUEEN ELIZABETH OR
FLOR DE CUBANA MADE BY
STEPHEN G. CONDIT OF
NEW YORK?

FACTORY AND OFFICE...
AVENUE D AND 10TH STREET

For Jamaica.—Head of Long Wharf. J. H. Freeman, agent.
For Portland.—Head of India Wharf. Charles F. Williams, agent.
For Provincetown.—Commercial Wharf. Atwood & Rich, agents, 109 Commercial Street.

The daily papers will give full information regarding the many summer excursion steamers, which leave at almost any hour of the day, during the season, for the various beach resorts.

Street cars pass all railroad stations and are to be found at or near every steamboat wharf, so that one can always be sure of cheap transportation from the place of arrival to the point of destination, or from one station or landing place to another; if not by one continuous line, at most with one transfer, while those who do not care to practice economy in this matter will find hacks and cabs waiting.

Baggage Transfers and Delivery.

On all the principal inward-bound trains, and at the wharves of incoming steamboats, there is a uniformed agent of the Armstrong Transfer Company. This official will take orders for the transfer of baggage to or from any point in the city, and passengers, on giving him their railroad baggage checks, will receive in return the company's "claim checks," which will give the owner security for his baggage, and these checks are to be surrendered only on receipt of the baggage at the specified destination.

This company also owns and operates a line of coupés, carriages, and diligences for the conveyance of passengers between stations, or to and from any part of the city, or for shopping or calling tours. The charge for delivering a trunk to any point within the city limits is 25 cents. The lowest charge for carriage hire for one person is 50 cents, which includes transportation for one trunk, to be taken on the carriage. It is well to bear in mind, however, that the driver of the carriage is not allowed to carry the trunk beyond the entrance hall of a private residence, and that if the trunk is to be carried upstairs it will be better to send it by the baggage delivery.

Outgoing Baggage.—An order should be left at the company's office, corner of Albany and Troy streets, or at any of the branch offices, at least two hours before the departure of train. They may be summoned by telephone from any part of the city to call at any hotel or dwelling for passengers or baggage, and the message is immediately transferred to the branch office nearest the place from which the order comes, and a carriage or baggage van is dispatched to the place of call. The owner of baggage forwarded to a station or steamboat landing is given the company's claim check on the baggage-room of the station or landing, by which his property is at once identified for checking.

This company will also check baggage through to destination, from a hotel or residence, if the parties desiring it have their railroad tickets. It has offices in all railroad stations, in all the principal hotels, and in different parts of the city.

Caution.—Never give up your checks to any but a uniformed train solicitor, or a regular office agent, or porter of either the transportation company which holds the baggage, or of the express company to which you intend to intrust it, and always take a receipt; and never give up your checks, if you claim your baggage yourself, to any person except the uniformed baggageman of the railway or steamboat line by which you have traveled. If you expect to meet or visit friends in the city who are residents, the best way, probably, is to keep your checks and let your friends manage the delivery of the baggage for you.

Getting About the City.

If one has but a short time to stop in the city, and desires to cover as much ground as possible in that time, it will be wise to engage a cab by the hour (on cab rates) and drive from point to point; but if several days can be devoted to " doing " the city such expense will be unnecessary.

Hacks and Cabs.—The *hackney-carriage and cab system* of the city is under the control of an official connected with the police department, the rates of fare being established by the city authorities, and vary according to the distance. Disputes about fares are unnecessary, as the drivers are required to display a rate-sheet when asked, and they are published in detail in the city directory. The fare for an adult for short distances, within specified limits in the city proper, is 50 cents; no charge is to be made for one trunk, but 25 cents is charged for each additional trunk.

Cabs furnish a cheap and brisk means of getting about the city. The charge is but 25 cents for transporting one person from any railroad station to a hotel, or from one railroad station to another. For one or more passengers from one point to another, within specified limits, the fare is 25 cents each. Cabs may also be hired by the hour for service within or about the city at the following rates: To or from any point within the limits of the city the rate shall be made on the basis of $1 per hour for one, two, three, or four passengers. The time shall be reckoned both going to and coming from any point, whether the cab returns empty or otherwise. Fractions of an hour shall not be charged after the first hour.

Cabs may be hailed anywhere on the street, when without a passenger, for any desired service. When " roaming " on the return from an engagement to the regular stand, it is customary for the driver to throw out a sign by the side of his seat with the suggestive words, " Not Engaged."

The following regulation applies to carrying children by carriage or cabs : For children under four years of age, with an adult, no charge shall be made. For a child between four and twelve years of age, when accompanied by an adult, the fare shall be half the price charged for an adult ; but when not so accompanied, or when a child carried in a cab is over twelve years of age, the charge will be for an adult fare.

Street-Car Routes.

By referring to the street-car routes, it will be seen that it is possible to visit all points of interest in Boston and the suburban districts without discomfort or great expense. The spacious open cars used in the summer, and the comfortable and equally roomy closed cars used in the winter and stormy seasons, afford a safe and pleasant means of transit. When the subway is finished and the congested condition of Washington and Tremont streets in their narrowest parts is relieved, transit will be much quicker. Nearly all the street-car routes have their points of attraction, and it would be impossible to give them all in a work of this kind. But in the following list an effort has been made to point out the way to those localities which are recognized as especially interesting and important:

A Few Attractive Routes.—

Dorchester via Grove Hall.—Green car marked " Dorchester " on dasher and end signs. Take car at corner Franklin and Washington streets.

Dorchester via Meeting House Hill.—Blue car marked " Meeting House Hill " on dasher and " Dorchester " on end signs. Take car at corner Franklin and Washington streets.

Forest Hills.—Green car marked " Egleston Square " on dasher and " Forest Hills " on end signs. Take car at Union Station, Scollay Square, or Old Granary Burying Ground. Forest Hills Cemetery is near the terminus of this route.

Franklin Park.—Green car marked " Grove Hall " on dasher and " Franklin Park " on end signs. Take car at Scollay Square, Old Granary Burying Ground, Washington Street, or Union Station.

Bunker Hill. — Green or yellow car marked " Roxbury and Charlestown " on dasher and " Franklin Street, Somerville," on end signs.

Cypress Street, Brookline.—Blue car marked " Brookline " on dasher and " Cypress Street " on end signs and top of car. Take car at Old Granary Burying Ground. Back Bay Fens and Brookline Park are on this route.

Jamaica Plain.—Yellow car marked " Jamaica Plain " on dasher and end signs. Take car at Union Station and Old Granary Burying Ground. This car passes near Jamaicaway and the Arnold Arboretum.

Davis Square, West Somerville.—Yellow car marked " Charlestown " on dasher and "Davis Square" on end signs. Take car at Scollay Square, Tremont Street, and Columbus Avenue.

Magoun Square, Somerville.—Yellow car marked " Charlestown " on dasher and " Magoun Square " on end signs. Take car passing Old Granary Burying Ground or at Scollay Square.

Milton.—Blue car marked " Field's Corner " on dasher and " Milton " on end signs. Take car at corner Franklin and Washington streets.

Field's Corner.—Blue car marked " Field's Corner " on dasher and end signs. Take car at Old Granary Burying Ground.

Neponset.—Blue car marked " Field's Corner " on dasher and " Neponset " on end signs. Take car at Union Station and Franklin, corner Washington Street.

City Point.—Red car marked " South Boston " on dasher and " City Point " on end signs. Take car at Union Station and Washington Street, between Adams Square and Boylston Street. This car goes to Marine Park.

City Point to Harvard Square. — Red car marked " South Boston " on dasher and " Harvard Square " on end signs. Take car at Park Square and Charles Street.

Malden.—Amber-colored car marked " Everett " on dasher and "Malden " on end signs. Take car at Scollay Square.

Medford.—Amber-colored car marked " Charlestown " on dasher and " Medford " on end signs. Take car at Scollay Square.

Woodlawn Cemetery.—Amber-colored car marked " Everett " on dasher and " Woodlawn " on end signs. Take car at Scollay Square.

Arlington and Arlington Heights.—Crimson car marked " Cambridge " on dasher and " Arlington " on end signs. Take car at Bowdoin Square. This route passes Harvard College.

Harvard Square to City Point.—Crimson car marked " Cambridge " on dasher and " Harvard Square " on end signs. Take car at Park Square and Charles Street. This car runs near Harvard College.

Harvard Square.—Crimson car marked " Cambridge " on dasher and " Harvard Square " on end signs. Take car at Old Granary Burying Ground. This route passes Harvard College.

Mount Auburn and Newton.—Crimson car marked "Cambridge" on dasher and " Mount Auburn and Newton " on end signs. Take car at Bowdoin Square. Mount Auburn Cemetery is on this route.

Reservoir, via Beacon Street.—Chocolate-colored cars marked " Reservoir " on dasher and end signs. Take car at Old Granary Burying Ground.

Reservoir, via Brookline Village.—Blue car marked "'Brookline " on dasher and " Reservoir " on end signs. Take car at Old Granary Burying Ground.

Oak Square.— Chocolate · colored cars marked " Allston " on dasher and " Oak Square " on end signs. Take car at Old Granary Burying Ground."

Free Transfers.—

The West End Street Railway Company issues free transfers as follows :

At Grove Hall.—For any car going south to Dorchester or Franklin Park ; and to any car going north on either Blue Hill Avenue or Warren Street.

At Dudley Street.—For any car going south on Warren Street or Blue Hill Avenue to Dorchester or Franklin Park ; north, to any car running on Washington Street, Shawmut Avenue, Tremont Street, Columbus Avenue, or Huntington Avenue to Scollay Square, Union Station, Charlestown or Somerville, and Bunker Hill.

At Roxbury Crossing.— To any car going toward Brookline, and to any Tremont Street car going north.

At Field's Corner.— For any Neponset or Milton car going south, or any Dorchester Avenue or Mount Pleasant car going north.

At East Boston Ferry, on the Boston side.— For any car going to East Boston or Chelsea.

At East Boston Ferry, on the East Boston side.— For any car running on Tremont and Washington streets.

At Dorchester Street, South Boston.— For any car going to City Point, Boston proper, or Washington Village.

At Broadway, corner Dorchester Avenue.— For any City Point to Harvard Square or Bay View to City Point car.

At Harvard Square, Cambridge.— For any car going to North Avenue, Mount Auburn, or Huron Avenue. Also to Park Square, Tremont House, Bowdoin Square, Scollay Square, via East Cambridge and City Point.

At Craigie Bridge.— For Claredon Hills, Somerville, Harvard Square, or Central Square, Cambridge ; City Point, South Boston, Park Square, Bowdoin Square, and Scollay Square.

At West Boston Bridge.— For Harvard Square, Brookline

Street, Pearl Street, Mount Auburn, and North Avenue. Also to City Point, South Boston, Park Square, and Bowdoin Square.

The **Lynn & Boston Electric Railroad System** covers the largest extent of territory of any electric railway in New England, and embraces a large area of the northern and northwestern section of Essex County, including Lynn, Saugus, Swampscott, Marblehead, Salem, Peabody, Danvers, Beverly, Wenham, and Hamilton; and, in Middlesex County: Stoneham, Wakefield, Melrose, Malden, and Everett. In Suffolk it runs through Boston, from Scollay Square, through Charlestown and Chelsea, to Revere, thence to Lynn, and so on. This system has 153 miles of single track (100 of which is single, with turn-outs), but it connects, outside of Boston, twenty-one cities and towns, with an estimated population of nearly 300,000. Lynn is the distributing center of this great electric system, and from this point the possibilities of change of direction seem to be limitless. The passenger station is at 71 Cornhill. The following is the official time-table:

To Beachmont, every sixty minutes.
To Chelsea, via Charlestown, every eight and ten minutes.
To Woodlawn Cemetery, every sixty minutes; (in summer), every thirty minutes.
To Revere, every thirty minutes.
To Revere Beach (in summer), every fifteen minutes.
To Lynn, Saugus, and *Swampscott*, every sixty minutes; Sundays (in summer), every thirty minutes.
Cars from *Lynn* to *Peabody* and *Marblehead*, every sixty minutes; to *East Saugus* and *Cliftondale*, every thirty minutes.

Ferries.

A list of the ferries which ply between Boston and the surrounding shores is as follows:

Chelsea Ferry (foot of Hanover Street).— First boat leaves Chelsea, foot of Winnisimmet Street, 4.15 A. M., 4.45; then every thirty minutes to 5.45 P. M.; then every fifteen minutes to 7.40 P. M.; then every thirty minutes to 11.15 P. M.; first boat from Boston, 4.30 A. M.; last boat, 11.30 P. M.; Saturday, fifteen minutes' time all day and evening.

Sunday.— First boat leaves Chelsea 6.15 A. M., every thirty minutes to 8.45 A. M.; every fifteen minutes to 7.45 P. M.; then every thirty minutes to 11.15 P. M.; last boat from Boston, 11.30 P. M.

East Boston (*North Ferry*), foot of Battery Street.— Leave at

HOTEL VENDOME — Commonwealth Avenue and Dartmouth Street.

4.07 A. M.; every fifteen minutes to 6 A. M.; every seven and one-half minutes to 11.22 P. M.; every fifteen minutes to 11.52 night; every twenty minutes to 4 A. M.

East Boston (*South Ferry*), foot of Eastern Avenue.—Leave at 4 A. M., every fifteen minutes to 6 A. M.; every seven and one-half minutes to 7.30 A. M., every six minutes to 11.30 A. M.; every nine minutes to 1.30; every six minutes to 6.45; every seven and one-half minutes to 8 P. M. (Saturday, 9 P. M.); every fifteen minutes to 12 P. M.; every twenty minutes to 4 A. M.

Boston & Revere Beach Railroad Ferry, 350 Atlantic Avenue. First boat leaves at 5.35 A. M.; every half-hour to 9.30 P. M.; then every hour to 11.30 P. M.

Hotels.

Boston is prepared to "welcome the coming and speed the parting guest" in such manner that he will long to visit her again. Her many good hotels are not confined, as in former days, to the business district of the city, but they are to be found in almost every quarter, and of various grades of excellence, and it would seem that "all sorts and conditions of men" might here find a temporary home which would meet their utmost requirements.

Hotels on the **American plan** furnish lodging, meals, and attendance at a fixed price per day, which varies according to the grade of the house and the location and appointment of rooms. Hotels on this plan are recommended to persons who, having command of their time, can be regular at meals, and to those who like to know in advance the expense to which they will be subject while in the city. The prices of these hotels vary from $2 to $5 a day and upward for extra rooms and other advantages. It should be borne in mind that proprietors charge travelers for the meal that is on the table when they arrive or when they depart. As there is usually a meal going on from the early breakfast until late in the evening, it is well for the guest to see that he is registered with his account beginning with the first meal which he intends to eat. If the clerk refuses to accede to this arrangement, the meal must be paid for or other quarters sought. In the list of hotels, which forms a part of this chapter, the lowest ordinary rates per day for one person are given for hotels run on the American plan. Higher rates are charged for superior rooms. Where the stay in the city is to be prolonged for more than one week, reduced rates may be obtained at some of these hotels by making arrangements before registering.

Hotels on the **European plan.**—In these hotels rooms are rented, with light and service, at so much per day, and the guest may take his meals in the restaurant attached to the hotel or elsewhere, as convenience or fancy may dictate. Hotels on the European plan will commend themselves to people who are limited as to time and do not have to consider expense. The prices range from 50 cents a night, in some of the cheaper hotels, to $2 and $3 in the Back Bay region; but very choice rooms and extra privileges must be paid for accordingly. As a rule, $1 per day for a single room and $2 for two persons together will secure accommodations that will satisfy most travelers.

Combination Plan.— Some of the best hotels combine both American and European plans, and in the list of minimum charges prices for both plans are given.

Extras.— The only extra charges which will be found in the bill will be for meals sent to private rooms, baths (when no bath-room is attached to the room occupied), and fires, or, in some cases, the turning on of steam heat. The fire is usually of hard coal, in an open grate, and costs from 50 cents to $1 per day, and 50 cents is the usual charge for baths. In almost every hotel will be found telegraph offices, barbers, and bootblacks, news-stands, and theater ticket offices; and in many, railway ticket offices and agents of the baggage transfer companies and carriage lines. These agents are authorized and may be patronized without hesitation.

Alphabetical List of Hotels.

Abbotsford, 186-188 Commonwealth Avenue.
Adams, 551-571 Washington Street — Eur., $1.
American, Hanover and Washington streets — Eur., $1.
Bellevue, 15-23 Beacon Street — Eur., $1.
Boston Tavern, 347 Washington Street — Eur., $1.
Brunswick, Boylston and Claredon streets — Am., $5; Eur., $1.
Clarendon, 521-523 Tremont Street — Eur., $—
Clark's, 575-581 Washington Street — Eur., $1.
Copley Square, Huntington Avenue and Exeter Street — Am., $3.50; Eur., $1.50.
Crawford, Scollay Square — Eur., $1.
Eastern, Canal and Causeway streets — Am., $2.
Falmouth, 66 Causeway Street — Eur., $1.
Hawthorne, 78 Pinckney Street — Am., $1.50.
Huntington, Huntington Avenue — Eur., $1.
Langham, 1679 Washington Street — Am., $2.50; Eur., $1.

Maverick, 23 Maverick Square, East Boston — Eur., $—
Oxford, Huntington Avenue and Exeter Street — Eur., $—.
Parker, School and Tremont streets — Eur., $1.
Plaza, Columbus Avenue and Holyoke Street — Eur., $1.
Quincy, Brattle Street and Brattle Square — Am., $3; Eur., $1.
Revere, Bowdoin Square — Eur., $1.
Reynolds, 623 Washington Street — Eur., $1.
Richmond, 254-258 Tremont Street — Am., $2.
Rockingham, 1202 Washington Street — Eur., $1.
Thorndike, Boylston and Church streets — Eur., $1.
United States, Beach, Albany, and Lincoln streets — Am., $2.50;
Eur., $1.
Vendome, Commonwealth Avenue and Dartmouth Street —
Am., $5.
Victoria, Dartmouth and Newbury streets — Eur., $1.
Winthrop, Bowdoin and Allston streets — Am., $2.50.
Young's, Court Street and Court Square — Eur., $1.

Notable Traits of Prominent Hostelries. — It is not the purpose of this book to make any discriminations, other than those which will aid the stranger to find a suitable home for his stay in the city. For addresses and rates, the foregoing list will give one a pretty good idea of what the town affords; but there are some traits that belong to the older hostelries which it will be desirable for the stranger to know before making his selection.

Most of the down-town hotels are in the district which is bounded on the north by Hanover Street and on the south by Boylston Street. In this district may be found every grade of hotel, and people who are here for business or sight-seeing will choose this locality for its convenience.

In the Back Bay district will be found places whose elegant appointments and air of refinement and exclusiveness will appeal to those who have the leisure and the means to command such luxuries.

The American House, on Hanover Street, between Portland and Court streets, is a long-established and very good hotel. It is interesting to know that upon a portion of the ground it occupies there formerly stood the home of Gen. Joseph Warren. This hotel has been in operation since 1835, and has had many alterations and additions. It was the first hotel to introduce the passenger elevator. Its prices are moderate, and it is a well-kept, comfortable house. It is largely patronized by business men, and by Western and Southern merchants.

The Adams House, at 553 Washington Street, is one of the largest and best hotels in the city. It is noted for the excellence of its cuisine, and for its display of good paintings, by modern artists, on the walls of its corridors and halls. It covers the site of the Lamb Tavern, built in 1745, and also of the first Adams House, built in 1844. Its central location and excellent service make it an attractive place to tourists.

The Hotel Brunswick, the *Vendome, Victoria*, and *Copley Square* hotels, in the Back Bay district, are, in all respects, the finest hotels in Boston. They are delightfully located in the fashionable part of the city, and have all the elegance of finish and appointment which the most fastidious guest can desire. All of these houses enjoy the patronage of wealthy and distinguished people, and are favorite places for private and club dinner parties.

The Hawthorne.— This house, which is located at 73 Pinckney Street, has long been a favorite boarding-place for teachers, artists, students, and business men and women. Within a few years it has been enlarged and is a most comfortable and well-kept family hotel. A limited number of transients find it an agreeable stopping place, and ladies of moderate means will here be as safe and sure of consideration as in their own homes.

The Parker House, on Tremont and School streets, was the first hotel established in this country on the European plan (first opened in 1855 by the late Harvey D. Parker), and it has always maintained the highest reputation for the comfort and elegance of its service. It has been enlarged at different times, and at present is a stately marble structure, covering a large area. The Tremont Street extension rises eight stories and terminates in a beautiful chateau roof. The Parker House has two large public dining-rooms, a café, and several private dining-rooms.

The Quincy House.— Not far from the American House, on Brattle Street, extending to Brattle Square, is the Quincy House, the oldest existing hotel in Boston. Established in 1819, and many times enlarged and remodeled, it has always been a favorite with travelers and business men. The rooms are comfortable and the prices moderate.

The Thorndike.—This is one of the leading hotels of the city. It is located on Boylston Street, facing the Public Garden, and runs through on Church Street to Park Square, opposite the Park Square Station of the New York, New Haven & Hartford Railway. It is elegantly furnished and has all modern improvements, and its location gives it the advantage of a transient patronage in its restaurants, as well as one of the best views of the Public Garden and Common to be had in the city.

The United States Hotel, on Beach Street, was built over half a century ago as a family hotel. Its location, while not in the most expensive and aristocratic part of the city, is convenient and accessible and near the center of the great wholesale and retail establishments, and is within a short distance of the Boston & Albany, and the New York, New Haven & Hartford and New York & New England Railway stations. It is one of the best hotels in the city, where much attention is paid to the comfort and pleasure of the guests.

Young's Hotel.—The main entrance to this hotel is on Court Avenue, and the hotel extends to Court Square and Court Street. It is one of the largest and best of the hotels on the European plan. One of the features of this hotel is the ladies' dining-room, the entrance to which is on the Court Street side. This is a handsomely decorated room 100 feet long and 31 feet wide. It connects with other large dining-rooms, and a café for gentlemen on the ground floor. This hotel is a favorite place with New Yorkers.

Restaurants.

There are several hundred establishments classed as restaurants in the business section of Boston. Of first-class establishments there are a number, and they include those at the leading hotels on the European plan. Recognized as among the best are those connected with Young's Hotel, the Parker House, and the Adams House. That of Young's Hotel is very extensive, occupying a large part of the ground floor of that establishment. It has dining-rooms for ladies and gentlemen, lunch rooms, and convenient lunch and oyster counters. The dining-rooms and café of the Adams House are first-class in every respect. In the Hotel Bellevue, on Beacon Street, is one of the best and prettiest cafés in town. At the Hotel Victoria, on Dartmouth Street, will be found another café with good service, elegant appointments, and fine cuisine.

Among the favorite places in the business section of the city is Marston's, on Brattle Street. Here, during the noon hour, hundreds of business men and women find rest and refreshment. This restaurant, since the improvements of 1894, is the largest public

3

restaurant in the city. Farther down town, about the Fanueil Hall markets, are several restaurants, largely patronized by market men, produce men, milk men, and down-town merchants, who find them satisfactory because of their fresh and wholesome fare.

On Water Street, near Washington, is found one of the most sumptuously appointed restaurants in the business section. It is known as Feners', and is but one of half a dozen such places managed by the same firm in different sections of the city.

In City Hall Square, Washington Street, and along Newspaper Row, are numbers of restaurants of every kind and grade. There are those in which refreshments can be secured at all hours of the day and night, and there are still others which cater mainly for the noon trade.

McDonald's, 132 Tremont Street, and 16 Winter Street, is popular with ladies who are shopping, and here they may obtain a light lunch at reasonable prices. At the noon hour the place is thronged with women, and a most animated scene is presented. Among other places of this character are *Weber's*, 25 Temple Place; *Dooling's*, 157 Tremont Street, and *Frost & Dearborn's*, 8 and 10 Pearl Street. *The Winter-Place Hotel*, on Winter Place, has recently succeeded Ober's French Restaurant, and it is, without doubt, one of the finest cafés in the city.

Hill's restaurant, corner of Washington and Boylston streets, is a popular place with the sporting classes, and here, at all times, may be found devotees of all branches of sport, disposing of a juicy chop and a mug of "musty" while discussing the current topics.

The leading French restaurants of the city are located on Van Rensselaer Place. *Vercellis'*, 61 La Grange Street, is the leading Italian restaurant, and is a place much patronized by fashionable Boston.

There are also a few good chop and oyster houses in this city. Of the former, two can be found on Essex Street and one in Avery Street, while of the latter class may be mentioned *Higgins'*, on Court Street ; *Brigham's*, on Washington Street, opposite Boylston Street, and *Bacon's*, on Essex Street.

The railroad restaurants of the city are, as a rule, good, and a well-cooked meal can be obtained at any of them on short notice.

Apartment Houses or Family Hotels.

Boston was the first American city to adopt this system of living, and it has become so popular that it would be impossible, in a work

THE CHARLESGATE — From the Back Bay Fens.

of this character, to mention any but the most prominent establishments. These houses range from palatial structures to plain, but comfortable, homes for people of moderate means, and they are to be found "down town" and in all residence districts. They are arranged in suites, the annual rent ranging from $400 to $3,000 and higher, according to size and number of rooms, elegance of finish, and location of the house. The rent includes · janitor service and steam heat. Many of the better class of these houses are furnished with elevators, and have the kitchens at the top of the building.

List of the Most Prominent Family Hotels.

Agassiz, 191 Commonwealth Avenue.
Berkeley, Berkeley, cor. Boylston Street.
Bristol, Boylston, cor. Clarendon.
Cluny, 233 Boylston Street.
Charlesgate, Beacon, cor. Charlesgate, East.
Gladstone, Belvidere Street.
Huntington, Huntington Avenue.
Nightingale, 637 Dudley Street.
Oxford, Huntington Avenue.
Pelham, Boylston, cor. Tremont.
Royal, 297 Beacon Street.
Tudor, Joy, cor. Beacon Street.

Boarding and Lodging Houses.

Those who contemplate spending some time in the city will find it possible to live, both economically and pleasantly, in a private boarding-house. Prices range according to location, size, and number of rooms required, etc., and one can obtain board in respectable neighborhoods at from $6 to $15 per week, according to accommodations. One can, of course, find lower and higher rates, but would hardly expect satisfactory table and rooms at less than $6.

Furnished Rooms.—A very pleasant method of living in Boston is to engage a furnished room by the week, and take one's meals at any of the numerous restaurants. This is an economical way of living, besides the freedom it gives for lunching or dining whenever and wherever one chooses. Rooms to be let for lodgings and private boarding-houses are advertised in the daily papers; but it will be well to require references of those having rooms to rent.

At the *Woman's Educational and Industrial Union* is kept a boarding-house directory, which ladies may consult at any time, and so learn of places whose respectability is guaranteed.

The *Young Men's Christian Association*, corner of Berkeley and Boylston streets; the *Young Men's Christian Union*, at 48 Boylston Street, and the *Young Women's Christian Association*, 40 Berkeley Street, are always glad to lend a helping hand to strangers, and also keep boarding-house lists, which are placed at the disposal of those needing such assistance.

II.
IN AND AROUND BOSTON.

The little jagged peninsula on which John Winthrop and his associates settled in 1630 was first called Shawmut, then Trimountain. The original area of Boston — 783 acres — has grown to 23,661 acres, and the census of 1895 will give Boston a population of over half a million. But these figures as to acreage and population are misleading and unfair. The increase in area has been the result of filling in the harbor and annexing adjacent towns. The first addition of outlying territory was made as early as 1637, when Noddle's Island " was layd to Boston " and given the name of East Boston. This addition, which more than doubled the area of the old town, remained a farm until 1833, when capitalists purchased most of the land, and improvements and settlements began. Early in the present century some parts of Dorchester were added to Boston, but it was not until late in the second half of the century that the municipalities of Roxbury, Dorchester, Charlestown, West Roxbury, and Brighton were absorbed by the ambitious metropolis.

Localities.

Early in the history of Boston it became the habit of the people to speak of the different sections of the town as the " North End," the " West End," the " South End," and then as the residence sections continued to stretch farther to the south and west and business interests absorbed the territory east and south of the Common and Public Garden, this came to be known as the Central District. This division of the city into districts is an advantage to those who are not familiar with the city's topography and points of attraction.

The North End is that part of the city lying north of State, Court, and Cambridge streets. This was once the wealthiest, most populous, and, in every way, the most important part of town.

Here were the great warehouses, the public buildings, and the homes of the old and prominent families. All this is now changed and this part of the city has been abandoned as a place of residence except by the poorest classes. All about this section are streets whose names will recall the historical association of the Colonial period. Many of the most suggestive names, however, were changed after the separation to suit the republican sentiments of the community. Thus King Street became State Street; Queen was changed to Court Street ; but Hanover, named in honor of the royal house, was for some reason permitted to stand. The latter is the main business thoroughfare of this district, starting from Scollay Square and running north to Aspinwall's Wharf. The street is mainly occupied by dealers in small wares, and has been appropriately called the " Bowery " of Boston. At one time the North End bore a bad reputation as a slum district, but since the population has become Italian and Hebraic rather than Celtic, it is more peaceful and orderly in its ways. The Italians predominate to the east and the Hebrews to the west of Hanover Street, and " Little Italy " and " New Jerusalem " flourish side by side in what was once the most aristocratic part of Boston. The Italian quarter has its own shops, banks, hotels, and restaurants, a theater, and two churches (St. Leonards of Porte Maurice, on Prince Street, and the Church of the Sacred Heart of Jesus on North Square).

Points of Interest at the North End.—The points which will be attractive to the traveler in this part of the city are the Old State House, on State Street; Faneuil Hall, in Faneuil Hall Square; Quincy Market, just across Merchants' Row from Faneuil Hall; Christ Church, on Salem Street; and Copps Hill Burying Ground, quite near the latter, on Hull Street. Each of these places is described in the chapter on " Old Landmarks," and in the chapter entitled " A Tour of the City " the most convenient way of visiting them is pointed out.

The Central District, or business quarter, lies east and south of Boylston Street, the Public Garden, the Common, Tremont, Court, and State streets. This region is frequently referred to nowadays as the " congested district," and into it are crowded banks, public buildings, warehouses, shops, offices, hotels, theaters, newspaper offices, and the railway stations.

The Subway.— By far the greater part of the interest that is now felt by Bostonians in the construction of the Subway centers in that section of the enterprise which affects the Common, the Public Garden, and Tremont Street, down to Scollay Square.

It begins in the Public Garden, just across the way from Church Street, or the Hotel Thorndike, and will be practically depressed until it comes to Charles Street, where it will commence to be a subway that, when completed, will not affect the surface. Its course will be under the Boylston Street mall of the Common to a point that is east of the old Public Library, where it will take a slight curve, so as to conform with the line of the Tremont Street mall of the Common, under which it will continue as far as Park Street Church.

Under the northeastern corner of the Common and the junction of Park Street with Tremont Street, there will be a loop for the use of the street cars, which are now turned around at the Granary Burying Ground. The main line will be sufficiently deflected to the eastward from the loop to bring it directly under Tremont Street, and thence it will follow a straight line to Scollay Square, and from there to its terminal at the Union Station. The southern end of the Tremont Street Subway will have an entrance near the junction of Tremont Street with Shawmut Avenue.

The West End includes that part of the city south and west of Court, Cambridge, Tremont, and Boylston streets, to the line of the Boston & Albany Railroad, following the line of that road to Brookline. Within these boundaries are the Common and Public Garden, Beacon Hill, and the Back Bay new land. Here is the fashionable part of modern Boston. The Back Bay quarter begins with Arlington Street next to the Public Garden. From Arlington Street three great thoroughfares—Newbury Street, Commonwealth Avenue, and Marlborough Street—run parallel with Beacon. These streets are crossed at right angles, at intervals of about 600 feet, by broad cross-streets, which are alphabetically named, a trisyllabic word alternating with a dissyllabic. *Commonwealth Avenue* is 240 feet wide and has a tree-lined parkway running through the center, with wide driveways on either side. It is one of the stateliest and most beautiful streets in the country. Within the limits of this district are many of the finest churches in the city proper. Some of the oldest societies in town have emigrated to the Back Bay,[1] and the more ancient parts of the city are comparatively bare of houses of worship.

The South End.—The section bounded on the north and west by Essex, Boylston, and Tremont streets, and the Boston & Albany

Railroad, and south by the old Roxbury line, is the South End of Boston, as the term is now understood. It is largely a district of residences, though *Washington Street* is principally given up to the retail trade, and considerable business is done on some other streets. A large part of this territory was reclaimed from the sea, and the South End is no longer a " neck of land."

Most of the streets, though generally pleasant, are drearily monotonous in their appearance. Their width and cleanliness, however, and their air of quiet and repose, give a pleasing appearance to this large residence quarter. The domestic architecture of this section exemplifies that peculiarity of Boston houses—the " swell front "—in great variety, but lacks the picturesque diversity of the Back Bay streets. Most of the houses are of brick, in long blocks, and they are sometimes beautifully adorned with woodbine or ivy.

The Annexed Districts.

East Boston is reached by street cars starting at Bartlett Street and running through Washington, Milk, Congress, State, Devonshire, Hanover, and Battery to the ferry. It is a place of piers, warehouses, dry docks, and marine railways ; of great mills, manufactories, oil works, fish curing and smoking establishments, and immense coal depots. At the Grand Junction Wharves several lines of trans-atlantic steamships load and discharge their cargoes, and here the Boston & Albany and the Boston & Maine railroads have extensive freight terminal sheds and grain elevators. The facilities at these wharves for the reception and dispatch of immigrants are superior to those of any American port. The immigrants who are to continue their journey by land into other sections of the country are carefully guarded from sharpers until they are sent away over the Grand Junction, which connects with the various trunk lines without passing through the city. Near the South Ferry are the Cunard docks, which have been established here since the organization of the line in 1840.

East Boston has its pleasant features and its historical associations. It has several parks, one of them — *Wood Island* — covering more than eighty acres, and affording from its higher points fine views of the harbor. *Belmont Square* is on the site of the old forts of 1776 and 1814. It is supposed that Noddle, after whom the island was originally named, was one of the colonists sent out by Sir William Brereton, who obtained a grant of this island from John Georges in 1628. When John Winthrop came to Boston in 1630, the land was occupied by Samuel Maverick, who lived here for twenty-five years, and who became the first slaveholder in the colony. East Boston was famed for its shipyards, which turned out some of the fast clipper ships, and in 1853, the largest sailing ship of its time. The " Great Republic " was built here. East Boston is connected with the mainland at Chelsea and Winthrop by bridges.

South Boston.— To reach South Boston by street car, take the red car marked " South Boston " on the dasher, and " City Point " on end signs. This car goes to Marine Park, and it may be taken at Union Station, and on Washington Street, between Adams Square and Boylston Street. From Park Square and Charles Street take a red car marked " South Boston " on dasher, and " Harvard Square " on the end signs.

South Boston is another great industrial center, having vast establishments in which naval cruisers are built and heavy ordnance made; immense cordage works, car-wheel works, elevator works, oil works, sugar refineries, and breweries. These establishments are mostly along the water fronts on the northern and southern sides. In the neighborhood of the Congress Street Bridge from the city proper are the Atlas stores, huge warehouses, the terminal piers of the New York & New England Railroad, and foreign and coastwise steamship docks. The district is thickly settled, and in the lower parts unattractive. Its pleasant places are on the hills beyond, and near and about City Point, the most easterly part, embellished by the Marine Park, the terminal of the noble chain of parks and parkways encircling the city.

Thomas Park, on Telegraph Hill, occupies the site of the " Dorchester Heights," on whose crest Washington planted the batteries which drove the British out of Boston in March, 1776. The spot is marked by a granite tablet. An institution which no visitor should fail to inspect is the *Perkins Asylum for the Blind*, which is described in Chapter VI, entitled " EDUCATIONAL INSTITUTIONS." This is located on East Broadway. On Old Harbor Street is *Carney Hospital*, described in Chapter VII. Of the *Marine Park*, attractive features are the promenades along the shore, and the great pier, commanding delightful views of the harbor, and the walks and driveway around Old Fort Independence on Castle Island, which is connected with the mainland by a bridge. The statue of Farragut, by

H. H. Kittson, was placed here in 1893. This is a great yachting station, and several clubs have their handsome club houses in the neighborhood. In the boat-building yards here many of the famous racers were built.

The Roxbury District. — Street cars for Roxbury pass Rowe's Wharf along Atlantic Avenue to Summer, Summer to Washington, Washington to Eliot, Eliot to Tremont, and Tremont to Roxbury Crossing. Another route is from East Boston Ferry via Hanover Street to Scollay Square, and thence via Tremont to Roxbury Crossing.

Roxbury was incorporated as a town but a few days after Boston, and when it became a part of Boston in January, 1868, its population numbered 28,400. In 1890 its numbers had increased to over 78,000, a growth of 50,000 in twenty-two years. It has a local history of which it is proud, but most of its interesting old landmarks have been swept away. It is now a pleasant residence quarter, with broad, shady streets, where most of the houses are detached. Among the points of interest is the meeting-house of the " First Religious Society of Roxbury," of which John Eliot, the apostle to the Indians, was the first pastor. This takes rank in age next after the First Church in Boston. It stands in Eliot Square, into which Dudley, Roxbury, and Highland streets converge, occupying the site of the first meeting-house. It was built in 1804, succeeding the fourth meeting-house on the spot, the one used for a signal station by the Continentals during the Siege of Boston. The architecture and the finish of the interior have been carefully preserved. The old Universalist Church, near by, stands where Gov. Thomas Dudley's house stood. The site of the earthworks thrown up in 1775, called the Roxbury High Fort, which crowned the Roxbury lines of investment during the siege, is marked by the Cochituate standpipe on the hill between Beech Glen and Fort avenues. This structure, erected and put in use in 1869, was intended to supply high service to those parts of the city which were at the higher levels, but it proved adequate to the supply of the whole city, and thus superseded the old reservoir on Beacon Hill. It has been rendered useless by the Parker Hill reservoir subsequently built. Around the interior pipe, but within the exterior wall of brick, a winding staircase leads to a lookout at the top. The site of the birthplace of Gen. Joseph Warren, on Warren Street, is marked by a tablet on the dwelling-house now occupying the spot. The old graveyard in which John Eliot is buried is on the corner of Washington and Eustis streets. Here, also, are the graves of other ministers of the First Parish in Roxbury, of the famous Dudley family, and of the father of Gen. Joseph Warren. The Dudley tomb is near the Eustis Street entrance. Among the worthy institutions of this district is the New England Hospital for Women and Children, on Dimock Street.

The Dorchester District. — To reach Dorchester via Meeting House Hill, take the blue cars marked " Meeting House Hill " on dasher, and " Dorchester " on end signs. These cars start from Franklin Street and run via Hawley, Summer, Washington, Eustis, Dearborn, and Dudley streets. To reach Dorchester via Grove Hall, take the green car marked " Dorchester " on dasher and end signs. These cars run via Washington, Summer, Hawley, Franklin, Washington, and Warren streets.

Dorchester, incorporated the same day as Boston, has, like Roxbury, an interesting local history. It became a part of Boston in 1870 and, in spite of its rapid growth, it has retained many of the features which have always made it a pleasant place for suburban residences. Its picturesque hills—Savin, Jones', Pope's, and Meeting House, and Mount Bowdoin—command extensive water and land views and are covered with costly villas. At Upham's Corner is the old burying ground (Dudley and Boston streets) where are the graves of Richard Mather, founder of the Mather family in this country, and others distinguished in the history of Massachusetts. At Five Corners—Massachusetts Avenue, Boston, Pond, and Cottage streets—is the old Everett House where Edward Everett was born. Meeting House Hill has been since 1670 the site of the successive meeting-houses of the First Parish (now Unitarian), dating from 1630. The present house, which was built in 1816, is a fair specimen of the church architecture of that period. At Field's Corner is the district post office and a branch of the Boston Public Library. The Lower Mills village is at the southerly bounds of the district on the Neponsit River.

The Charlestown District.—To reach Charlestown via Bunker Hill, take green or yellow car marked " Roxbury and Charlestown " on dasher, and '"Franklin Street, Somerville," on end signs. Horse cars for Charlestown may also be taken on Tremont Street, north of Temple Place, via Scollay Square. Charlestown was annexed to Boston in 1873, and, although smaller in area than some of the other

additions, it is one of the richest localities in historical associations.
Most of its points of interest can be compassed in a short walk; but
the one which towers above all the others is *Bunker Hill Monument*,
on Breed's Hill, where the battle celebrated in song and story was
fought. The monument marks the lines of the old redoubt and is
built of coarse granite, thirty feet square at the base, rising, majestic-
ally, 220 feet. From the observatory at the top a wide view of the
surrounding country may be obtained. This is reached by a spiral
flight of stone steps inside the shaft, and the visitor who intends to
make the ascent will be interested to know that there are just 295
of these steps. In the building at the base of the monument are
interesting memorials of the battle, and an excellent statue of General
Warren, in marble, the work of Henry Dexter. The spot where
Warren fell is marked by a stone in the grounds near by. The
bronze statue of Colonel Prescott, in the main path, occupies the spot
where he is supposed to have stood at the opening of the battle. The
Bunker Hill Monument was begun in 1825, and the corner stone was
laid by Lafayette. Daniel Webster delivered the oration at this
ceremony, and also on the occasion of the dedication of the completed
work, June 17, 1843.

The *Navy Yard* at "Moulton's Point" is where the British troops
landed for the fight at Bunker Hill. Its present area is about eighty-
seven acres, and within the inclosure are large and costly buildings.
The grounds are attractive, with two broad avenues running through
them. There are extensive parks for cannon and shot, a parade
ground, marine barracks, store and ship houses, arsenal and magazine, a hammered granite dry dock, a long rope walk, a museum, a
library, and the homes of the commandant and other officers.

The yard is open daily to visitors. Passes can be obtained at the
main gate at the junction of Wapping and Water streets. Another
feature of the district is the ancient burying ground on the west side
(Phipps Street, off Main Street), in which are the graves of Rev. John
Harvard, the first benefactor of Harvard College ; of Thomas Beecher,
the ancestor of the famous Beecher family in America, and of others
prominent among the early settlers. The monument in this graveyard to the memory of Harvard, a simple granite shaft, was set up in
1828. It bears the following inscription in Latin :

"That one who merits so much from our literary men should no
longer be without a monument, however humble, the graduates of

the University of Cambridge, New England, have erected this stone, nearly 200 years after his death, in pious and perpetual remembrance of John Harvard."

In City Square, the municipal building (the City Hall before annexation) marks the sight of the "Great House" of the Governor, in which the Court of Assistants named Boston. Charlestown is distinguished as the birthplace of Samuel F. B. Morse, the inventor of the electric telegraph.

The West Roxbury District includes Jamaica Plain, and is the largest and most picturesque of the annexed sections of the city. Within its limits are the greater parks of the public parks system — Jamaicaway, along the ornamented banks and graceful shores of Jamaica Pond; the Arnold Arboretum; and Franklin Park, the crowning feature of the system; the Bussey Institute, and beautiful Forest Hills Cemetery. Jamaicaway may be reached from the city proper by electric cars to Jamaica Plain; the Bussey and the Arboretum by electrics through the Roxbury District to Forest Hills, or by the Providence division of the Old Colony Railroad to the Forest Hills Station; and Franklin Park by the last-mentioned routes, or by electrics to Eggleston Square, in the Roxbury District. The Bussey and the Arboretum are on the west side of the railroad, and Forest Hills and Franklin Park on the east side.

The Brighton District. — (For street cars to this district see Reservoir and Oak Square routes under heading: "A Few Attractive Routes," in Chapter I.) This is a region of breezy, commanding hills, of broad and attractive streets, and pleasant homes. Two magnificent boulevards from the Back Bay — Commonwealth Avenue and Beacon Street — extend into it, and one of the most popular drives is to *Chestnut Hill Reservoir* (connected with the Boston Water Works), a pleasure resort which lies within its limits. A beautiful driveway, from sixty to eighty feet in width, surrounds this work, in some parts running close to the embankment, and in others leaving it and rising to a higher level, at a little distance from which a view of the entire reservoir can be had. The work covers more than 200 acres. It is a double reservoir, being divided by a watertight dam into two basins. The surface of water in both is about 125 acres, and when filled to their fullest capacity the basins hold about 800,000,000 gallons.

Metropolitan Boston.

Lying within a radius of ten miles of the City Hall, Boston, are thirty municipalities whose interests are so closely identified with those of the city proper, and so continuous is the population of these sections that it is difficult to draw a boundary line and say where one leaves off or another begins. Within this metropolitan district are the eleven cities of Cambridge, Lynn, Somerville, Chelsea, Malden, Newton, Waltham, Quincy, Everett, Medford, and Woburn, and in these cities and the adjoining towns are the homes of thousands of people whose business interests are in Boston, and who daily come to their work in the city. Many of these towns and cities are already organized into administrative districts. Thus the Boston Postal District comprises seven municipalities, the Sewerage District contains eighteen municipalities, and the Park District, thirty-seven municipalities. The last extends beyond the limit of metropolitan population on account of including some important landscape features. Legislation is now under consideration which looks to the establishment of a metropolitan water district to furnish these cities and towns with an adequate supply of pure water from the Nashua River, at an estimated cost of nearly $20,000,000. To this metropolitan district is aptly given the name of " *Greater Boston,*" and a "Greater Boston Commission," appointed under recent legislation, is engaged in the consideration of some form of metropolitan organization, which, with self-governing powers and a federalized government for general interests, will still leave the various municipalities independent in authority in purely local matters. Each of these cities has its distinguishing and interesting features; all have a great variety of manufacturing industries, and several are famous in special lines — as Woburn for its tanneries, Waltham for watches, Lynn for shoes, and Chelsea for rubber goods and art tiles. All have charming residence quarters and are connected with the central city by fine boulevards and parkways. In a work of this kind it is only possible to give the prominent features of those localities which will prove of especial benefit to the tourist.

Brookline lies south of the great Back Bay region of Boston, and is approached by the stately boulevards of that quarter. It has been called the most beautiful example of a city's suburb in the world. Here are delightful walks and drives among charming villas and park-like estates. At Clyde Park are the club-house and grounds of the *Country Club*, an organization of Bostonians, members of leading clubs in town. Within the grounds are tennis courts, and one of the best racing courses in the neighborhood of the city, and the club-house is a hospitable country mansion of the olden time.

Cambridge, with over 80,000 inhabitants, is the largest of the out-lying municipalities. Famous, in the first place, as the seat of the great university, it has many associations and points of interest, which attract all who are so fortunate as to visit Boston. The *Old Elm*, under which Washington stood when he took command of the Continental Army on July 3, 1775, is still standing at the junction of Mason and Garden streets. Not far away, on the Watertown road, near Brattle Street, is the stately house where the General made his headquarters — the mansion of the Royalist, Col. John Vassal, who abandoned it at the outbreak of the war. In after years it was the home of Longfellow — from 1837 until his death in 1882. Farther on is Elmwood, the birthplace and home of James Russell Lowell. The historic old mansion-house is set in the midst of trees and shrubbery, and dates from about 1760. The poet's study, where he wrote nearly all his poems, was on the third floor.

Beautiful *Mount Auburn*, the last resting-place of so many of America's great men and women, is partly in Cambridge and partly in Watertown. It is fully described at the end of this chapter.

Cambridge is also noted as being the first place in this country where a printing-press was set up. In 1639 a press was brought over from England and put in operation in the house of the President, who had charge of it for many years. The first thing printed upon it was the Freeman's Oath, followed by an Almanack for New England, and the Psalms. A fragment of the last-named work is preserved in the college library, and copies of it may still be seen in some anti-quarian libraries. Cambridge has at the present day some of the largest and most completely furnished printing-offices in America, conspicuous among which are the Riverside Press and the University Press. Noteworthy among the public buildings of Cambridge, and conspicuous pieces of architecture, are the *City Hall*, on Main Street, and the *Public Library*, on Broadway and Irving Street. Both these buildings and the lot·on which the library stands, known as Library Common, were gifts to the city from Frederick H. Rindge of Los Angeles, Cal., a former resident of Cambridge. The public

4

Manual Training School, on Irving Street, opposite the library, was also established and equipped for use by Mr. Rindge.

Newton, the "Garden City," ranks next to Brookline as a beautiful suburb. It is reached by the Boston & Albany Railroad or by street cars. (See "Attractive Routes," Chapter I.) Between Riverside Station and Waltham, on the Charles River, is the principal fresh-water boating ground.

Somerville is the third of the suburban cities in population. Its points of historic interest are Prospect Hill and Winter Hill, where a redoubt and breastworks were constructed by the Americans in 1775, and in the "Old Powder Tower" will be found an interesting Colonial relic.

At **Medford,** the seat of Tuft's College, which occupies College Hill, are many fine old houses, conspicuous among them being the Craddock house, the oldest building in New England.

Lynn, the second of the suburban cities in population, is the largest shoe-manufacturing town in the United States, and the seat of the greatest electric industry. Its seaside and rural surroundings are very beautiful, and the neighborhood of its fine beach is a delightful residential section. Lynn Woods, with 2,000 acres, is the second largest public pleasure-ground belonging to any city in the country.

Salem, sixteen miles northwest from Boston, is reached by the Boston & Maine Railroad, or by the Boston & Lynn Street Railway. It is an extremely interesting old city, abounding in historical associations. Tourists will be interested in the old *Roger Williams house*, which is still standing at the corner of North and Essex streets, and which is noted as the building in which some of the persons charged with making use of the dark art of witchcraft were examined. *Gallows Hill*, where the execution of witches took place, is in the western part of the city. But the associations clustering about the scenes of Hawthorne's romances are more potent in their attraction for tourists than even historical facts. The house on Mall Street, where Hawthorne wrote "The Scarlet Letter," is standing. The Custom House desk of pine, where he made his first rough draft of "The Scarlet Letter," is sacredly preserved in the reconstructed old First Church. Another building, the Ingersoll house, dating from 1662, is called "The House of the Seven Gables," although Hawthorne declared that he drew entirely upon his imagination for the site of his Puncheon mansion.

STATUE OF MINUTE MAN — Concord Battle Field.

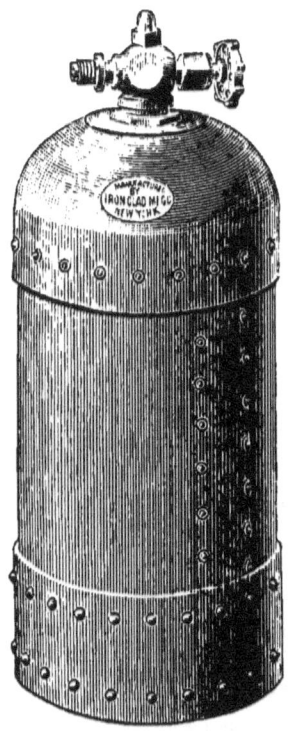

Salem is the county seat of Essex County. A State normal school is located here, and among other institutions are the Essex Institute and the East India Marine Hall. The latter contains the fine ethnological museum of the Marine Society.

Of the suburbs south of the Dorchester District, *Hyde Park* is attractively set in the Neponset Valley; *Milton* is a town of quiet beauty and park-like character, including the wild and picturesque Blue Hills, the greatest elevations in Eastern Massachusetts, which command far-reaching coast and inland views. *Quincy* is famous as the birthplace of two presidents of the United States and the home of several notable families. Its old stone church contains the tombs of the presidents. The public library, known as the Crane Memorial, designed by Richardson, is among its features.

Concord is a picturesque old town, nineteen miles from Boston, and it may be reached by either the Fitchburg Railway, or the Lowell division of the Boston & Maine Railway. Tourists will find here many objects of historical and literary interest. Concord is revered, not only because

> " By the rude bridge that arched the flood,
> Their flag to April's breeze unfurled,
> Here once the embattled farmers stood
> And fired the shot heard round the world,"

but because here lived Nathaniel Hawthorne, Thoreau, Emerson, and the lamented Louise Alcott.

On the shore of Lake Walden, one of the most beautiful sheets of water in New England, is a pile of stones marking the spot where was located the hut in which Thoreau lived for some time. Hawthorne wrote in his note-book:

" The scenery of Concord, as I beheld it from the summits of the hills, has no very marked characteristics, but has a good deal of quiet beauty in keeping with the river. There are broad and peaceful meadows, which I think are among the most satisfying objects in natural scenery. The heart reposes on them with a feeling that few things else can give, because almost all other objects are abrupt and clearly defined; but a meadow stretches out like a small infinity, yet with a secure homeliness which we do not find either in an expanse of water or air. The hills which border these meadows are wide swells of land, or long and gradual ridges, some of them densely covered with woods."

The places which the visitor will especially enjoy seeing are the
" Old Manse," the Concord Monument, the graves of the British
soldiers who fell in the memorable battle of April 19, 1775, and the
Davis Museum of relics in the Old Court House.

Cemeteries.

The cemeteries now in use are all situated in the outskirts of Boston.   The city, several years ago, forbade, by ordinance, all burials in
graves within the old city limits.   The ancient burying grounds are
described in the chapter on " Old Landmarks."

The following is a list of the cemeteries now in use in the city, or
which have offices in the city:

Catholic Cemetery, Roxbury District, Fenwick Street.

Cedar Grove, Dorchester District, between Milton, Adams, and
Granite streets.

East Boston Cemetery, East Boston, Swift, corner Bennington
Street.

Evergreen Cemetery, Brighton District, near Chestnut Hill
Reservoir.

Forest Hills Cemetery, Jamaica Plains District, Morton Street.

Gethsemane Cemetery, West Roxbury District, Brook Farm,
Baker Street.

Hand-in-Hand Cemetery, West Roxbury District, Grove Street.
A Hebrew burying ground.

Israelitish Burying Ground, East Boston, Byron, corner Homer
Street.

Mount Auburn Cemetery, in Cambridge and Watertown.

Mount Benedict Cemetery, West Roxbury District, Arnold
Street.

Mount Calvary Cemetery, West Roxbury District, Mount Hope
Street, near Canterbury.

Mount Hope Cemetery, West Roxbury District, Walk Hill Street.

St. Augustine Cemetery, Dorchester Street, South Boston.

Warren Cemetery, Roxbury District, Kearsarge Avenue.

Woodlawn Cemetery, Everett.

The only cemeteries which have more than a local interest are
Mount Auburn and *Forest Hills.*

Mount Auburn Cemetery, the most widely-known burial-place in
this country, is partly in Cambridge and partly in Watertown.   It is
reached by street cars marked " Cambridge " on dasher, and " Mount
Auburn and Newton" on end signs, which, starting from Bowdoin
Square, pass along Green, Chambers, and Cambridge streets, West
Boston Bridge, Main and Harvard streets, Harvard Square, and
Brattle Street.   This beautiful resting-place of the dead was

consecrated in 1831. Containing about 125 acres, it has more than thirty miles of avenues and paths. This is the oldest garden cemetery in the United States, and was first established by the Massachusetts Horticultural Association, in connection with an experimental garden. The place was first known as Stone's Woods, and was much frequented on account of its rural attractions. The diversified surface, with its wooded hills, quiet vales, and verdure-wreathed ponds, gives unusual opportunities to the landscape architect. On the top of the highest hill is a stone tower, from which an extensive view of the surrounding country is to be had. Mount Auburn is the shrine to which many pilgrims come, because of the eminent dead who are buried here.

Passing through the Egyptian entrance gate, and following the first roadway to the left, we reach, after a short walk, the grave of James Russell Lowell, under the shade of a tall hornbeam tree. The grave is simply marked by an old-fashioned slate slab, with angel's head and wings, and bears the following inscription:

Sacred to the memory
of
JAMES RUSSELL LOWELL.
Born 1819.   Died 1891.
And of his wife,
MARIA WHITE.
Born 1821.   Died 1853.
And also of his second wife,
FRANCES DUNLAP.
Born 1825.   Died 1885.

Near by are the names of two of his children : Blanche, "a lily of a day," 1847, and Rose, 1849-1850.

Ascending the path just beyond to Indian Ridge, directly behind Lowell's grave, at the entrance to Catalpa Path, we stand before a sculptured marble sarcophagus bearing the single name, **Longfellow**. On the same ridge is Motley's grave, in the Motley family lot. Following Catalpa Path, but bearing to the west and crossing Central and Cyprus avenues, we come to the granite Sphinx, by Martin Milmore. This masterly work, the gift of Jacob Bigelow, in 1872, stands in front of the Gothic granite chapel, and is a memorial of those who died for the Union. Leaving the Sphinx and following Cyprus to Walnut Avenue, we approach the tower before mentioned. In the neighborhood of the tower, on Walnut Avenue, is the red stone sarcophagus of the great orator, Rufus Choate. Near the tower are also the graves of Edwin Booth (Anemone Path), Charlotte Cushman (Palm Avenue), Charles Sumner (Arethusa Path), and Edward Everett (Magnolia Avenue). Near the base of the tower is Pyrola Path, leading from Walnut Avenue to the Fuller lot, on which is the monument raised to the memory of Margaret Fuller and her husband, the Marquis Ossoli of Italy. Just beyond, on Bellwort Avenue, is the grave of Aggassiz, marked by a rough-hewn granite boulder, brought from the glacier of the Aar in Switzerland. The grave of Phillips Brooks is on Menoza Path, from Spruce Avenue, a short walk from the chapel.

Other interesting graves are those of President Jared Sparks, historian (Garden Avenue); Anson Burlingame (Spruce Avenue), John G. Palfrey, historian (Sweetbriar Path); President Josiah Quincy, (Sweetbriar Path), "Fanny Fern," sister of N. P. Willis (Eglantine Path, leading from Fir to Spruce); James T. Fields (Elder Path, leading from Walnut to Spruce), Rev. William Ellery Channing (Greenbriar Path, leading from Pine Avenue), and Henry F. Durant, founder of Wellesley College (Osier Path, leading from Willow Avenue to Indian Ridge Path).

Of the statuary at Mount Auburn, that within the chapel is the most noteworthy—the figures, in marble, of John Winthrop, by Horatio Greenough, modeled in 1856; of James Otis, by Thomas Crawford, of the same date; of John Adams, by Randolph Rogers, 1859; and of Joseph Story, by his son, William W. Story, 1853. The bronze statue of Nathaniel Bowditch, at the left of the avenue leading from the entrance gates to the chapel, is by Ball Hughes.

Forest Hills Cemetery.—This beautiful cemetery is near the Forest Hills Station of the New York, New Haven & Hartford Railway, Old Colony division. It is also reached by the Forest Hill line of electric cars. The gateway, constructed of Roxbury stone and Caledonia freestone, is a unique piece of work. On the front, in golden letters, is the inscription :

I AM THE RESURRECTION AND THE LIFE.
And on the inner face —
HE THAT KEEPETH THEE WILL NOT SLUMBER.

The grounds of the cemetery are very picturesque, with hills and dales, woods and greensward, and pretty sheets of water. Among its interesting memorials, on the summit of Mount Warren, is the tomb of Gen. Joseph Warren, the hero of Bunker Hill ; on Dearborn Hill is the monument of Gen. H. A. S. Dearborn, who laid out the grounds ; the grave of Rear-Admiral Winslow, in Orange Path, marked by a block of rough granite from Kearsarge Mountain ; a granite monument marks the grave of Rear-Admiral Henry Knox Thatcher, on Tantana Path ; in near neighborhood are the graves of William Lloyd Garrison (on Smilax Path), James Freeman Clarke (Ageratum Path), and J. M. Manning, pastor of the Old South Church from 1857 to 1882 ; in close neighborhood, also, are graves of John Gilbert, the actor (Brook Path), and E. L. Davenport (Arethusa Path), the latter marked by a marble memorial, placed by his daughter, Fanny Davenport, in 1880. The grave of Oliver Ditson, the music publisher, is marked by Thomas Ball's beautiful ideal figure of St. John. In the Soldiers' Lot is the Soldiers' Monument, erected by the city of Roxbury, and designed by Martin Milmore. The most notable piece of sculpture in the cemetery is the memorial to Martin Milmore and his younger brother, James, who died several years before him. It is on Cypress and Poplar avenues, and is the work of Daniel C. French. It represents the Angel of Death staying the hand of the sculptor, and it received a medal of the third class in the Paris Salon of 1891.

III.

THE CITY'S PARKS AND SQUARES.

The Common.—Of the many urban parks and squares the one which will first claim the attention of the visitor is the dear old Common, which, since the settlement of the town, has been set apart for the use and pleasure of all the people. In 1640 a vote was passed by the town that, with the exception of "3 or 4 lotts to make up ye streete from bro Robte Walkers to ye Round Marsh," no more land should be taken from the Common, and the power of this vote, and the loyalty of the citizens in upholding it, kept the Common sacred to the uses of the people. When the city charter was adopted the right to alienate any portion of the enclosure was withheld from the city government.

In the early days the Common was used as a pasture and training field; but that the people enjoyed it then very much as later generations do is shown by the following extract from an "Account of Two Voyages," published in London in 1675: "On the south there is a small but pleasant Commons, where the gallants, a little before sunset, walk with their *Marmalet*-Madams, as we do in Moorfields, etc., till the nine o'clock bell brings them home to their respective habitations, when presently the constables walk their rounds to see good orders kept, and to take up loose people." Before and long after this the Common was the usual place for executions. People accused of witchcraft, murderers, pirates, and other malefactors here met their doom. But in 1812 a memorial, signed by a large number of citizens, induced the selectmen to order that the Common should no longer be used for such a purpose. The level ground east of Charles Street has been used from the very earliest times as a parade-ground. Here take place the annual parade and drumhead election of the

BEACON STREET MALL   THE COMMON

Ancient and Honorable Artillery Company, the oldest military organization in the country, and here the Governor delivers to the newly elected officers their commissions for the year.

The present area of the Common is about forty-eight acres, bounded by Tremont, Park, Beacon, Charles, and Boylston streets. It is inclosed by an iron fence, and, with its broad and shaded walks and grand old elms, it is a veritable blessing to those who cross it for business or pleasure ; in summer, a green and quiet refuge into which one may escape from the glare, the heat, and the rush of the town ; and in winter in its snowy drapery affording equally beautiful and restful views. One of the conspicuous objects in the Common, standing near the Park Street mall, is the *Brewer Fountain*, the gift to the city of the late Gardner Brewer, Esq., which began to play for the first time on June 3, 1868. It is a copy in bronze of a fountain designed by the French artist Liénard, executed for the Paris World's Fair of 1855, where it was awarded a gold medal. The figures at the base represent Neptune and Amphitrite, Acis and Galatea. The *Soldiers' and Sailors' Monument*, on the hill by the *Frog Pond*, occupies historic ground. Here the British constructed a redoubt during the Siege, when the Common, with earthworks on its highest points, was the British camp. The platform of the monument, thirty-eight feet square, rests on a solid bed of masonry sixteen feet deep. The four bronze statues, on the projecting pedestals, represent Peace, a female figure bearing an olive branch, with eyes turned to the south; the sailor, carrying a drawn cutlass, looking toward the sea; History, another female figure holding a tablet and stylus, and looking upward; and the soldier, a federal infantryman, the best figure on the monument, standing at ease. The four large bronze reliefs between the pedestals represent " The Departure for the War," " The Sanitary Commission," " The Return from the War," and " The Departure of the Sailor from Home." The main shaft of the monument, a Roman-doric column of white granite, rises from the pedestal between the statues. The four allegorical figures at its base represent the North, South, East, and West. The shaft is crowned by a female figure, eleven feet high, representing the " Genius of America." In one hand she grasps the American flag, in the other a drawn sword and laurel wreath. The monument bears the following inscription, written by President Eliot of Harvard College:

TO THE MEN OF BOSTON
WHO DIED FOR THEIR COUNTRY
ON LAND AND SEA IN THE WAR
WHICH KEPT THE UNION WHOLE
DESTROYED SLAVERY
AND MAINTAINED THE CONSTITUTION
THE GRATEFUL CITY
HAS BUILT THIS MONUMENT
THAT THEIR EXAMPLE MAY SPEAK
TO COMING GENERATIONS.

The monument was designed by the late Martin Milmore, and cost the city $75,000. It was dedicated with great pomp on September 17, 1877.

The monument by Robt. Kraus, which commemorates the "Boston Massacre of 1770," stands near the Tremont Street mall, between the West Street gate and Boylston Street. On the front of the granite shaft is a figure typifying " Revolution Breaking the Chains." The bas-relief on the base represents the scene of the massacre as it was presented in an old plate published in London, with a " Short Narrative." On one corner of the relief are these words :

From that moment we may date the severance of the British Empire. — DANIEL WEBSTER.

and on the other corner :

On that night the foundation of American Independence was laid. — JOHN ADAMS.

On the shaft are cut the names of the victims of the massacre. The monument, erected by the State, was dedicated on November 14, 1888, on which occasion the late John Boyle O'Reilly was the poet.

On the Boylston Street side of the Common is the old Central Burying Ground, which is described in the chapter entitled " Old Landmarks."

The Public Garden, containing about twenty-four and a quarter acres, was formerly a " marsh at the bottom of the Common," and from 1791 to 1819 was occupied by ropewalks, the land having been granted by the city for this purpose. These ropewalks were burned in the latter year, and, the lands having become valuable, their owners were about to divide and sell the tract in lots for dwelling and business purposes. This aroused the citizens, who made such effective resistance that, in 1824, the city bought for $55,000 what it had given away in 1791. It was then decided to establish a public garden here, but the matter lagged for several years and little was done until 1859, when an act of the Legislature and the vote of the city finally settled the question. In 1839 a number of citizens established a Botanic Garden near the corner of Beacon and Charles streets. The garden was successful for a few years, until its conservatory was destroyed by fire. The irregular artificial pond in the center of the garden contains a trifle less than four acres, and was constructed in 1859. It is spanned by a ponderous iron and stone bridge, which has been styled by the local wits the " Bridge of Size." The city annually makes liberal appropriations for the maintenance of the garden. It contains many varieties of ornamental trees and shrubs, and in the season of flowers thousands of bedded plants are displayed.

The sculpture exhibited in the Public Garden does not particularly enhance its beauty. The best piece of work is the equestrian statue of Washington, by Thomas Ball, which stands in the central path, near the Arlington Street entrance. This statue, which it took the sculptor three years to model, was unveiled January 29, 1869. It is considered one of the half-dozen really great equestrian statues which the world possesses. There are few people to-day who appreciate the size of the statue. The extreme length of the group is 16 feet, height 16 feet; the height of the figure of Washington is 12 feet. The pedestal, of Quincy granite, was designed by Hammet Billings, and is 15 feet in height and 18 feet in length. The total cost of the work was $42,000. It was cast by Silas Mosman of the Ames Manufacturing Company at Chicopee. The reader may form some idea of its size when he knows that a tall man may stand under the barrel of the horse. To see it to advantage, one ought to be at least 100 feet away from the statue.

Near the Washington Statue is a fountain, whose basin is adorned by a marble " Venus Rising from the Sea." The fountain is so arranged as to throw, when in action, a fine spray over the figure. Another monument on the Arlington Street side of the garden commemorates " The discovery that the inhaling of ether causes insensibility to pain." This monument, the work of J. Q. A. Ward, was the gift of Thomas Lee, and was dedicated in June, 1868. It is of granite and red marble, and the ideal figures surmounting the shaft illustrate the story of the " Good Samaritan." The bas-reliefs represent, respectively, a surgical operation, the patient under the influence of ether, the Angel of Mercy descending to relieve suffering humanity, a field hospital, with a wounded soldier in the care of the surgeons, and an allegory of the Triumph of Science. On the Beacon Street side of the garden is the *Statue of Edward Everett*, by W. W. Story. The fund for this statue was raised by a public subscription in 1865, and the statue was presented to the city in 1867. The sculptor has endeavored to represent Everett in the attitude of the orator as he spoke the words, " Washington, the guiding star."

The bronze statue of Charles Sumner, on the Boylston Street side, represents the statesman in the act of speaking, with a roll of manuscript in the left hand, the right hand extended downward in a gesture. This statue is also the work of Thomas Ball, the sculptor of the Washington. It was erected in 1878, at a cost of $15,000, raised by subscription. Near the Sumner Statue is one of Thomas Cass, the brave colonel of the 9th Massachusetts Volunteers. This is the work of Stephen O'Kelley, and it was presented to the city by the Society of the 9th Regiment.

The New Public Park System.

One of the grandest features of Boston is her " Public Park System," which, when completed, will form an almost unbroken chain of parks and parkways from Craigie's Bridge, at the north end, to City Point, South Boston. The park commissioners have expended over $11,000,000 upon the city's parks, squares, and parkways, and no people in the world are so bountifully supplied with beautiful and accessible pleasure-grounds. Every section of the city is included in this provision, and the neighboring cities and towns are not to be left behind. Thus, Cambridge is building a system of riverside and other parks; Newton, Malden, Waltham, Brookline, Quincy, and Hyde Park have fine park works in construction; Lynn has a public forest of 2,000 acres in Lynn Woods, and, in addition to these, there is the great Metropolitan system. This includes 3,200 acres of wilderness at Middlesex Fells, 4,000 acres at the Blue Hills, 475 acres at Stony Brook Woods, a small reservation at Beaver Brook, the projected Mystic Valley Parkway, the banks of the Charles to be preserved and improved, and a magnificent ocean shore reservation contemplated at Revere Beach and Winthrop. Altogether, in the Metropolitan Parks District, Greater Boston already has between 13,000 and 14,000 acres devoted to public uses for park and water supply purposes.

STONY BROOK BRIDGE — Back Bay Fens.

5

Geo. D. Brown & Co.

Wholesale and Retail Dealers in

Mutton
Lamb
Veal
and # Poultry

Stall 15, Faneuil Hall Market

Boston...

Telephone, 894 Haymarket.

Lambs' Tongues
A
Specialty.

George D. Brown.
Herbert C. Brown.

The first link in the green chain encircling the city is **Charlesbank**, which lies along the river front on Charles Street, between Cragie's and West Boston bridges. It is a broad promenade, about 600 feet long, bordered by trees and shrubs, and provided with public gymnasiums and baths for the people's use, and with playground and sand courts for the children. Charlesbank is ultimately to be extended for miles along the river and past the Fens.

The Fens.—The area of the Fens is about 115 acres, artistically laid out with roads, bridle-paths, and footpaths along the waterway. The main entrance to the Fens is by the way of Commonwealth Avenue beyond Massachusetts Avenue. Here is Miss Whitney's ideal statue of Leif Ericsson, the Norse discoverer of America. The inscription reads :

> Leif
> The Discoverer,
> Son of Erik,
> Who sailed from Iceland
> And landed on this continent
> A. D. 1000.

The farther end of the Fens affords wide expanses of meadows, trees, and shrub-planted slopes. Of the bridges which span the waterway, the stone Boylston Street bridge was designed by the late H. H. Richardson. The Fens opens the parkway, which under various names—as Audubon Road, Fenway, Riverway, Jamaicaway, and Arborway—winds through Longwood and Brookline, along the Muddy River, Leverett Pond, Ward's Pond, and Jamaica Pond, to the Arnold Arboretum and Franklin Park.

Leverett Park.—This section of the parkway, lying between Tremont and Perkins streets, comprises sixty acres of land in Boston and fifteen acres in Brookline, and contains Leverett Pond, of twelve acres, Ward's Pond, of 2.7 acres, Willow Pond, and a number of smaller ponds or pools, most of the latter being provided for the proposed Natural History Garden which it is expected that the Boston Society of Natural History will sometime establish here. The practical completion of this park opens to use a most varied and attractive pleasure-resort, with the scenery of a sloping valley rising gradually from the lake at its lower end to a considerable eminence at its head, with numerous smaller ponds compassed with verdant banks and woodsides, among which wind the paths, ending in the sylvan seclusion of Ward's Pond, which nestles in a deep depression between the wooded knoll and the high ridge of Perkins Street.

Jamaica Park, comprising about 120 acres, which encircles Jamaica Pond, is one of the loveliest stretches of landscape in the park system. The pond covers seventy acres, and affords an ideal place for boating in the summer and for skating in the winter. The grounds are laid out in walks and drives, shelters are provided, and the Pinebank Refectory is a delightful place for refreshment. The views across the water, with its gently curving, wooded shores, are enchanting and worth traveling many miles to enjoy. And all this beauty is within a half-hour's drive of the center of the city. Take the electric cars for Jamaica Plain, and, leaving the car at the corner of Center and Pond streets, walk a short distance to the west to the beautiful Jamaicaway and revel in the charms of this lovely park.

The Arnold Arboretum, the largest and finest tree museum in the world, is a place of great natural beauty. It was formerly a part of the estate of Benjamin Bussey, which he bequeathed to Harvard University for a school of agriculture, horticulture, and veterinary science. The Bussey Institute was opened in 1870, and two years later the Arboretum was established. It was named in honor of James Arnold, a wealthy merchant of New Bedford, who left the Arboretum $100,000. The Arboretum contains 167 acres, of which 122 belonged to the Bussey estate. Under an agreement between the university and the city (to hold for 999 years), the university maintains and develops the Arboretum, and the city constructs and cares for its roads and paths and polices it. It has broad, pleasant driveways, winding footpaths, and a magnificent piece of the primeval forest.

Franklin Park embraces about 600 acres of picturesque country, whose natural beauties have not been disturbed in the process of opening and developing the territory for public use. The broad drives wind among woods and glades, through quiet valleys, and along breezy uplands from which delightful views of town and country can be enjoyed. Among its attractive features are, on one side, the great " Playstead," the " Greeting," and the " Deer Park "; on another side the " Wilderness," and on the " Country " side " Ellicottdale," the " Dairy," and " Sheepfold."

Roomy and comfortable carriages stand near the theater at Blue Hill entrance, and for 25 cents one may take a seven-mile drive over perfect roads, which take in all the points of interest in the park. A

AGASSIZ BRIDGE — Back Bay Fens.

bridge to carry the Forest Hills entrance over the traffic road, leading from Forest Hills Street to the cemetery, has been built, thus making the connection of the Arborway with the drives of Franklin Park complete.

Ellicott House, at the entrance to the playgrounds of Ellicottdale, has been opened to the public this season. Toilet, bath, dressing, and check rooms are provided for use in connection with the tennis courts to be laid out at Ellicottdale. It is expected that a branch of the electric railroad will be extended from Washington Street, through Williams Street to a point near Ellicott House, and thence through Forest Hills Street and the new traffic road to Forest Hills Cemetery; thence by way of Morton Street to Washington Street, near the Forest Hills Station. This loop will bring passengers to the gates of the park on its western border, where are situated its most picturesque picnic grounds and rambles, and the new playground, and will, when constructed, be a great convenience to visitors.

A refectory is being built on the hill near the junction of Blue Hill Avenue and Glen Lane, where the old Gleason House formerly stood. The plans provide for a brick and terra-cotta structure, 121 feet long by 69 feet wide, containing on the ground level a large restaurant, private dining-room, service-rooms, toilet-rooms, and staircases leading to a roof-garden, which forms, in effect, a second story, having pavilions 21 feet square upon each corner, containing stairs, serving, and toilet room. These pavilions are connected by covered galleries on three sides, the remainder of the space being open to the sky.

A collection of fancy pigeons, including archangels, blondinettes, English owls, fantails, tumblers, magpies, nuns, and turbits, from the estate of the late Edmund Quincy at Isle au Haute, was presented to the department by Dr. H. P. Quincy, and are domiciled at the propagating house in the nursery at the southerly end of the park. They are a source of much attraction to visitors. A flock of about 200 sheep also attracts considerable notice, and is a popular feature of the park, the herding of the sheep by the shepherd dogs being an interesting sight.

Scarboro Pond, seven acres in area, adds very materially to the attractiveness of the park. Its summer level, which gives it a depth of eight feet, will, in winter, be lowered to a depth of four feet to

make it safe for skating. Eventually a boating and skating house
will be built here.

The beautiful parkway drive ends at Franklin Park, but begins
again in the *Dorchesterway*, which, in connection with the proposed
strandway, will open into Marine Park.

Marine Park, on South Boston Point, includes historic *Castle
Island*, and is connected with the latter by bridge. From its south-
eastern extremity an immense pier, 1,300 feet in length, has been
built out into the bay, and is a crowded resort on pleasant Sundays.
A head-house was built at the shore end of the point. This building is flanked on two sides by raised platforms to serve as promenades, which will extend to the iron pier, and below and between
which 500 bath-houses will be located. The house will contain
a general waiting-room on the ground or terrazzo floor, with
men's and women's waiting and dressing rooms and bath toilets, the
spaces under the promenades being devoted to offices for the police
and a foreman's and workmen's room. On the second floor two large
cafés, connected by a corridor and service-rooms, adjoin the promenades, the rest of this floor being occupied with the upper part of
the general waiting-room and the stairway to the restaurant, which
is on the third floor above the waiting-room. Over the cafés are the
kitchen and store-room, and the attic contains the laundry.

Castle Island has been a fortified spot since 1634. Castle William,
which stood here when the Revolutionary War broke out, was burned
by the British when they evacuated Boston. The Continentals then
took possession of the island and restored the fort. In 1798 its name
was formally changed to Fort Independence, and the following year
it was ceded to the United States. From 1785 to 1805 it was the place
of confinement for prisoners sentenced to hard labor, provision having
been made in the act of cession to the United States that this privilege should be retained. The present fort was built about the year
1855.

A Park for the North End. — The agitation for a park for the
thickly populated region north of Hanover Street resulted, in 1894, in
the passage of an act by the Legislature authorizing the park board to
take lands to a limit of $300,000 in assessed values, and providing
$50,000 for construction. Soon after its passage the board examined
the locality with a view of determining the most suitable location for
the proposed pleasure-ground, with regard both to natural advantages

and a fair amount of territory for the desired purposes. As a result of this examination the commission secured a small tract for which a complete plan has been prepared, which may be described as follows: The land to be devoted to purposes of recreation lies between the ancient Copps Hill Burying Ground and the sheet of water which is the confluence of the Charles and Mystic rivers. It is separated from the burying ground by Charter Street, and it is crossed by the busy waterside thoroughfare called Commercial Street. Between the two streets the narrow public domain slopes steeply down between two ranks of tenement houses, thus opening a prospect from the already frequented Copps Hill. Between Commercial Street and the water the original shore-line has disappeared under a tangle of more or less ancient sea-walls, fillings, and pile structures.

The plan is designed to make this confined space afford opportunity for the greatest possible variety of modes of recreation. Thus, a resting-place commanding a view of the water is provided upon a broad terrace on a level with the upper street; an ample promenade adjacent to the water is provided upon a pier, the upper deck of which will be reached from the terrace by a bridge which will span Commercial Street; a good place for children to play is provided on a beach, which will form the shore of the small haven to be formed by the pier; dressing-rooms will be provided for the use of bathers, floats, and other conveniences for boatmen. The stone terrace and its accompanying flights of steps will be plainly, but substantially, constructed, while the steep earth-slopes at the ends and below the high wall will be planted with low shrubbery. The foot-bridge spanning Commercial Street will be a light steel truss. The new or restored beach will terminate against sea-walled piers of solid filling, from the end of one of which the long and substantial pleasure pier will run out to and along the harbor commissioners' line. Between the beach and Commercial Street there is room for a little greensward and a screening background of shrubbery.

IV.

OLD LANDMARKS.

To meet the requirements of a great and growing modern city, many of the interesting old landmarks of Boston have been sacrificed. But much remains for the edification and instruction of tourists who are interested in historical relics. Faneuil Hall, the Old State House, the Old South Church, Christ Church, and King's Chapel are shrines which attract and inspire all true Americans, and many a pleasant and profitable hour may be spent in reviewing their history and associations as well as in visiting them.

In no other American city are there so many objects which will awaken reverent regard for that past which is the birthright of America's sons and daughters. Economy of time and strength should be considered in all sight-seeing, and, as most of the interesting historical landmarks of Boston are in the north part of the town, this is not difficult to attain. A pleasant half-day may be spent in doing the Old State House, Faneuil Hall, Quincy Market, which is just across Merchants' Row from Faneuil Hall; Christ Church, and Copps Hill Burying Ground. Another half-day should be given to the Old South Meeting-House, King's Chapel, King's Chapel Burying Ground, the Old Granary Burying Ground, and the Central Burying Ground on the Common. In the following pages will be found a brief historical and descriptive sketch of each of these places.

Faneuil Hall, in Faneuil Hall Square, is the "Cradle of Liberty" to all who have studied the history of the United States. The first Faneuil Hall was built in 1742, and was a market-house. It was given to the town by Peter Faneuil, a wealthy merchant of French descent, who stipulated that it should be legally authorized and maintained under proper regulations. The enlargement of the plan to include a second story for a hall was a later thought. When the people voted to accept the building they provided that it should be

(52)

called Faneuil Hall "forever." The first Faneuil Hall was a structure only 100 feet long by 40 feet wide. It was partially destroyed by fire in 1761, only the walls remaining, but rebuilt by the town the following year. Part of the funds used in rebuilding were raised by a lottery authorized by the State. The second building was completed and formally opened on March 14, 1763, and it was the patriot James Otis, then the orator, who dedicated the hall to "the cause of liberty." Here were held all the town meetings, and, in the dark days before the Revolution, the patriot orators of the time often spoke the words which inspired and kept moving the spirit of Liberty.

This building, which was only about half the size of the present one, and two stories high, remained so until 1805. Then, under the direction of Bulfinch, it was much enlarged and improved. Its width was increased to 80 feet; the third story was added; the hall was made 78 feet square and 28 feet high; large galleries, resting on Doric columns, were put in, and the large platform was built. The large painting which hangs at the back of the platform represents Webster addressing the United States Senate on the occasion of his celebrated reply to Hayne. It is by Healey, and is interesting because of the portraits of some of the leading public men of that day. Other portraits hanging on the walls of Washington by Stuart, Faneuil by Col. Henry Sargent, Hancock (Copley), Samuel Adams, John and John Quincy Adams, and Warren (all by Copley), Commodore Preble, Andrew, Lincoln, and Everett, by modern artists, are mostly copies, the originals having been removed from the hall to the Art Museum for safe-keeping.

Until the town became a city, in 1822, the town offices were established here, and it was the regular place of town meetings. Some of the greatest orators and agitators of the country have been heard from its platform. It was here, in 1837, that Wendell Phillips made his first anti-slavery speech.

The hall is never let for money, but is at the disposal of the people whenever a sufficient number of persons, complying with certain regulations, ask to have it opened. The city charter contains a wise provision forbidding its sale or lease. It is freely opened to visitors. On the upper floor of the building is the armory of the Ancient and Honorable Artillery Company, the oldest military organization in the country. It contains quite a museum of colonial and provincial relics, which is also open to visitors.

Old State House.—On Washington Street, at the head of State Street, is the Old State House, one of the few survivals of the ante-Revolutionary buildings in the city. It is, undoubtedly, the most interesting historical building in this country, for it was here that "the child Independence was born." On this site, where had been the earliest market-place of the town, the first town house was built in 1657. This house was destroyed by fire in 1711, rebuilt a year later, and again burned in 1747. The present structure was built in 1748, and within and without the building many stirring events have occurred. It was in turn town house, court house, province court house, State house, and city hall. On the first floor was, in early times, the merchants' walk or exchange. In the eastern room of the second story, with an outlook down King Street, was the council chamber, where the royal governors of the province and the royal council sat. The western chamber was the general court-room. Over the entrance to one of these two rooms is placed the seal of the city, and over the other that of the State.

During the Stamp-Act excitement the stamped clearances were burned in front of its doors. The British troops were quartered within the building in 1768, and within a few feet of its eastern porch occurred the Boston massacre, on March 5, 1770. The next day Sam Adams stood in the council chamber and made his successful demand upon the royal representatives for the immediate removal of the troops from Boston. Forthingham, in describing this event, says: "On the walls of the chamber were representatives of the two elements now in conflict—of the Absolutism that was passing away, in full-length portraits of Charles II and James II robed in the royal ermine; and of a Republicanism which had grown robust and self-reliant, in the heads of Endicott, and Winthrop, and Bradstreet, and Belcher. Around a long table were seated the lieutenant-governor (Hutchinson) and the members of the council, with the military officers; the scrupulous and sumptuous costumes of the civilians in authority—gold and silver lace, scarlet cloaks, and large wigs—mingling with the brilliant uniforms of the British army and navy. Into such imposing presence were now ushered the plainly-attired committee of the town." In the same room Generals Clinton, Howe, and Gage held a council of war just before the battle of Bunker Hill.

From the balcony on the State Street side, where the royal procla-

THE OLD STATE HOUSE — State, Devonshire, and Washington Streets.

mations had been delivered, the news of the Declaration of Independence was proclaimed. Inside the house "the gentlemen stood up, and each, repeating the words as they were spoken by an officer, swore to uphold the rights of his country." The proclamation was followed by a banquet in the council chamber. In 1789, at the western end of the building, Washington reviewed the great procession in his honor on the occasion of his last memorable visit to Boston. Here, in 1835, William Lloyd Garrison found refuge from a mob, which had broken up an anti-slavery meeting and threatened the life of the brave agitator.

When the State House was no longer needed as a public building it was remodeled and turned into business offices. The original architectural effect was wholly destroyed by the addition of a mansard roof and other changes. But in 1880–81 public-spirited citizens began a movement which ended in the successful restoration of the building. From the second story upward the exterior of the house now has the appearance it wore in the Provincial period. The gilt eagle, with the State and city arms spread over the western front, was placed to appease over-sensitive citizens who were disturbed by the restoration of the lion and unicorn, in copies, on the eastern gables.

Every effort has been made to reproduce the old interior, as well as exterior, and restore, in every detail, the architecture of the Colonial period. The halls have the same floors and ceilings, and on three sides the same walls, that they had in 1747. One end wall in each of the two chambers is new, but it rests upon the same spot as the old wall. The balcony of the second story has been restored upon the model of the still-existing attic balcony, and it is reached through a window of twisted crown glass, out of which have looked all the latter royal governors of the Colony and the early governors of the State. The windows of the upper stories are modeled upon the small-paned windows of Colonial days ; but four-paned windows have been put in the first floor and basement to satisfy the tenants, these portions being let for business purposes. On the second floor are two main halls and several ante-rooms. The whole of the second floor, the attics, and cupola are leased by the city to the Bostonian Society. The terms of the lease provide for an annual payment by the society of $100, and the maintenance of the rooms for public exhibition. An interesting collection of antiquities, relating to the building itself, and to the early history of the city and State, with several portraits, and quaint, crude paintings of ancient date, is exhibited here. Admission free.

Old South Meeting-House, on Washington Street, corner of Milk Street, has been called the "Sanctuary of Freedom." The ground on which it stands was the place where Governor John Winthrop had his home, and here he died in 1649. The land was afterward owned by Madam Mary Norton, wife of Rev. John Norton, who gave it in trust "forever for the erecting of a house for their assembling themselves together publiquely to worship God." The Old South Society worshiped here from 1669 to 1875, when they moved to their new place of worship on Boylston Street. The first meeting-house was a small cedar building, erected in 1670, and in this building Benjamin Franklin was baptized. In 1730 the present brick structure took the place of the first meeting-house. Although a place of worship, the old meeting-house had, at times, served other purposes. In the stirring times that preceded the Revolution, when Faneuil Hall was too small to hold the town meetings, the church opened its doors to the patriotic crowds.

When the British occupied the town they desecrated the place and injured the building by using it as a place for cavalry drill. The fire of 1872 came very near to the precious building, but it escaped destruction, and it then served as a post office until the completion of the post office wing of the Government building. In 1876 the building was sold to be torn down and replaced by a business block. But the "Old South Preservation Committee," composed of twenty-five Boston women, came to the rescue and purchased it conditionally for $430,000. The meeting-house is now used as a loan museum of historical relics, which include many interesting portraits, quaint old furniture, flags, and weapons. It is open daily, and the entrance fee (25 cents) becomes a part of the preservation fund. It is still sometimes used for public meetings; and the regular "Old South Lectures to Young People," on local history, given by eminent men, are features of the winter seasons. The tablet on the tower was placed in 1867:

Old South
Church gathered 1669
First House built 1670
This House erected 1729
Desecrated by British Troops 1775-6.

The Old Corner Book Store.—After leaving the Old South it would be well for the visitor to cross Washington Street, and, going one block to the north, on the corner of School Street, he will find the oldest building now standing in Boston. On this ground was once the dwelling of Ann Hutchinson, the strong-minded woman who was banished for heresy in 1637. The present building bears the date of 1712, and was the property of Thomas Crease, who used it as a dwelling and apothecary shop. It was occupied by different tenants, as a dwelling or for offices, until 1816, when Dr. Samuel Clarke, whose son, Rev. James Freeman Clarke, was born here, restored the old building to its original purpose of a drug store. Doctor Clarke was succeeded in 1828 by Messrs. Carter & Hendee, who first used the front as a book store, and it has been devoted to this purpose ever since. It has been occupied successively by the firms of Carter & Hendee, Allen & Ticknor, William D. Ticknor & Co., Ticknor & Fields, E. P. Dutton & Co., A. Williams & Co., and, lastly, by its present tenants, Damrell & Upham. Through some of these firms it may be said to have become the progenitor of the great publishing houses of Houghton, Mifflin & Co., Roberts Brothers, and of the music business of Oliver Ditson. Here James T. Fields, James R. Osgood, and Benjamin H. Ticknor began their careers as clerks, and here many of the famous writers and students of Boston love to gather and exchange greetings and ideas as they lingered in the quaint old building which has watched the coming and going of so many generations.

King's Chapel, on Tremont Street, corner of School Street, is a plain and solid edifice of dark granite, with a massive square tower, surrounded by wooden Ionic columns. The interior of the church, with its rows of columns supporting the ceiling, the richly painted windows of the chancel, the antique pulpit and reading-desk, the mural tablets, and quaintly sculptured marble monuments that line the walls, will impress the visitor with its likeness to old English churches.

The first King's Chapel was built in 1689 by the first Episcopal Church Society of Boston. This society had previously worshiped first in the town house and then in the Old South, under the protection of Governor Andros, and to the great sorrow of the Congregationalists. The first chapel was built of wood. In 1710 the building was enlarged. Pews were reserved for the Governor and British army and naval officers. The walls and pillars were hung with the

6

escutcheons of the king and royal governors, and upon the pulpit stood an hour-glass to mark the length of the sermons. An early description of Boston states that " King William and Queen Mary gave them a pulpit-cloth, a cushion, a rich set of plate for the communion table, and a piece of painting, reaching from the bottom to the top of the east end of the church, containing the Decalogue, the Lord's Prayer, and the Apostles' Creed."

The present chapel was completed in 1753. The plan embraced a steeple, but none was ever built. During the reign of Queen Anne it was called Queen's Chapel, and for a while after the Revolution the name was changed to Stone Chapel; but in time the love of the people for ancient local names caused them to return to King's Chapel, which has been retained ever since. After the evacuation the chapel remained closed until late in the year 1777, when the Old South Society, whose meeting-house had been so nearly destroyed by the British troops, occupied it, using it for nearly five years, while its own meeting-house was undergoing repairs. In 1782 the church was reopened by the remnant of the old society, with James Freeman as " reader;" and under his teaching the Unitarian faith was professed by the congregation, so that what had been the first Episcopal church in Boston became the first Unitarian. In 1787, Doctor Freeman was ordained rector, and thereupon the connection of the church with the American Protestant Episcopal church was terminated.

Christ Church, Salem Street (North End), was built by the second Episcopal Society in Boston, and is the oldest church edifice now standing in the city. It was dedicated December 29, 1723, and its first rector was Rev. Timothy Cutter, D. D., who served until his death, August 7, 1765. This old church is a very interesting landmark, as it retains, generally, its original appearance. This is the church from whose steeple it is supposed the lanterns of Paul Revere were hung out to warn the country of the march of the British troops on Lexington and Concord. A tablet on the front of the church, placed there October 17, 1578, bears this inscription :

> The signal lanterns of Paul Revere displayed in the steeple of this church, April 18, 1775, warned the country of the march of the British troops to Lexington and Concord.

But some very good authorities claim that this is a mistake, and that the North Church referred to by Paul Revere, in a narrative

CHRIST CHURCH, "OLD NORTH"—Salem Street.

which he prepared twenty years after the events, was the North Church, then standing in North Square. But Christ Church was also known as the "North Church," and, to support its claim, brings evidence which shows that Capt. John Puling, one of the wardens of the church, received the signal to display the lanterns, and that Robert Newman, the sexton, hung them out.

The original steeple was blown down in the great gale of 1804; but the present one was built immediately after the fall of the old, and is an accurate reproduction of that. Aside from the steeple there is nothing in the plain exterior of the church to attract attention.

The interior retains most of its ancient fixtures and the original decorations have been reproduced. The high, small-paned windows, with deep seats; the balcony supported by pillars, the top "slaves' gallery," and the old-fashioned pews, have all been preserved. The bottom of the old pulpit, of hour-glass shape, is still there; but the upper part was given away by one of the church officials in 1820, and a modern affair fills its place. The organ is not the original one, which was imported from London in 1756, but it is inclosed in the original antique case. The clock below the rail has been doing duty since 1746. The figures of the cherubim in front of the organ and the chandeliers were taken from a French vessel by the privateer "Queen of Hungary," in 1746, and presented to the church by Captain Grushea ; its Bible, prayer books, and communion service, still in use, were given to it by King George II in 1733, and the silver bears the royal arms. The chime of bells, the sweetest and most musical the town has ever had, was brought from England in 1744. It is said to be the first chime in America.

Old Burying Grounds.

The four oldest burying grounds in the city proper are still preserved and faithfully cared for, though for several years they have been unused as places for burial. They are among the most interesting of the landmarks of early times, and speak eloquently to us of many of the founders of Boston.

King's Chapel Burying Ground, on Tremont Street, between King's Chapel and the building of the Massachusetts Historical Society, is the oldest of these ancient cemeteries, and for thirty years was the only burial place of the town. The exact date of its establishment is not known, but according to Shurtliff's "Topographical and Historical Description of Boston," the first burial here was on the 18th of February, 1630. The following reference to it is found in John Winthrop's record : " Capt Welden, a hopeful younge gent & an experienced souldier dyed at Charlestowne of a consumption, and was buryed at Boston wth military funeral." Here rest the remains of Gov. John Winthrop and his son and grandson, who were governors of Connecticut; of Governor Shirley, Lady Andros (the wife of Governor Andros); John Cotton, John Davenport, the founder of New Haven, Conn.; John Oxenbridge and Thomas Bridge, pastors of the First Church, and other well-known personages of the early days. In one of the tombs here were deposited the remains of the wife of John Winslow, who, as Mary Chilton, according to tradition, was the first woman to touch the shore at Cape Cod, springing from the boat as it approached the shore. There are many quaint old gravestones in the yard; but some of them have been moved from their original positions and set up as edgestones to paths. One of these stones has a most remarkable history. At some time the stone was removed from the grave it marked and was lost. In 1830, when some excavations were being made near the Old State House, it was found several feet below the surface of State Street. It is of green stone and is inscribed :

HERE : LYETH
THE : BODY : OF : M<small>R</small>
WILLIAM : PADDY : AGED
58 YEARS : DEPARTED
THIS : LIFE : AUGUST THE [28]
1658.

On the reverse is this singular stanza of poetry :

HEAR . SLEAPS . THAT
BLESED . ONE . WHOES . LIEF
GOD . HELP . VS . ALL . TO . LIVE
THAT . SO . WHEN . TIEM . SHALL . BE
THAT . WE , THIS . WORLD . MUST . LIUE
WE . EVER . MAY . BE . HAPPY
WITH . BLESED . WILLIAM . PADDY.

Copps Hill Burying Ground, on Hull Street, a short distance from Old Christ Church, was the second burial place established in Boston. It was first used for interment in 1660, and was several times enlarged. Here are the graves of Doctors Increase, Cotton and Samuel Mather ; Rev. Dr. Andrew Eliot of the New North Church, Mrs. Mary Baker, a sister of Paul Revere ; Chief Justice

Parker, and many who were prominent in the early history of the town. During the Siege the inclosure was occupied by the British as a military station. The soldiers used the gravestones as targets, and the marks of the bullets may yet be seen on some of them. A stone which seems to have been particularly sought out by the soldiers in their desecration of the ground bears the following record :

Here lies buried in a
Stone Grave 10 feet deep
Capt. DANIEL MALCOM Mercht
who departed this Life
October 23d 1769
Aged 44 Years
A true Son of Liberty
a Friend to the Publick an
Enemy to oppression and
one of the foremost in
opposing the Revenue Acts
on America.

Captain Malcom would be called a smuggler at the present time, for the above inscription refers to his landing a valuable cargo of wines without paying duty upon it. But as the tax was regarded as unjust and oppressive, the citizens approved and lauded the act. The oldest stone in the graveyard is believed to be one bearing date of 1661, erected to the memory of the grandchildren of William Copp, for whom the hill was named — an industrious cobbler who lived near by. Several stones bear earlier dates, but these were altered from the original, the date 1690 in one case having been changed to 1620, and 1695 to 1625. One of the oldest stones records the death of "Captain Thomas Lake, who was perfidiously slain by ye Indians at Kennebec Aug. 14, 1676." Captain Lake was a commander of the Ancient and Honorable Artillery Company in 1662 and 1674, and, according to the story, the slit deeply cut in his gravestone was filled with the melted bullets taken from his body. The metal was long ago chipped away by relic hunters. There are several slabs bearing armorial devices, which the superintendent of the yard is always ready to point out to visitors. During the summer months the gates are thrown open, and the people are allowed access to the cool, shaded grounds. At times, when the gates are closed, admission can be obtained by application to the superintendent, who lives in the neighborhood. The high, rough stone wall was placed when it became necessary, in the improvement of this section of the city, to cut down that portion of the hill without the limits of the burying ground.

Old Granary Burying Ground, on the north side of Tremont Street, between Park Street Church and the site of the old Tremont House, is the most interesting of the old burying grounds of Boston. It was established in 1660, at the same time that the Copps Hill Burying Ground was laid out. The ground was formerly a part of the Common, and it received the name it bears because of its proximity to the old town granary, which· stood where the Park Street Church now stands. The list of the distinguished dead who rest here includes nine governors of the Colony and State; three of the signers of the Declaration of Independence; Paul Revere, the patriot; Peter Faneuil, the donor of the market house and hall that bears his name; Judge Samuel Sewall, six doctors of divinity, the first mayor of Boston, and many others. Upon the front of one of the tombs, on the side next to Park Street Church, was once a marble slab with the inscription, " No. 16, Tomb of Hancock ;" but nothing now marks the resting-place of the first signer of the Declaration of Independence, and the first Governor of Massachusetts under the Constitution. In another part of the yard is the grave of Samuel Adams, " the father of the Revolution." Near the Tremont House corner are the graves of the victims of the " Boston massacre of 1770." The most conspicuous monument here is one erected in 1827, which marks the graves of the parents of Benjamin Franklin. It contains the epitaph, composed by their illustrious son, " in filial regard to their memory." This is the inscription :

> They lived lovingly together in wed lock fifty-five years, and without an estate, or any gainful employment, by constant labor and honest industry maintained a large family comfortably, and brought up thirteen children and seven grandchildren respectably. From this instance, reader, be encouraged to diligence in thy calling, and distrust not Providence.
> He was a pious and prudent man ;
> She a discreet and virtuous woman.

The names of some of the distinguished persons buried here are displayed upon the bronze tablets fixed upon the gates of the main entrance to the yard. The high, carved gateway, in the summer time is picturesque in a mantle of ivy. Entrance to the yard may be obtained upon application to the superintendent. Inquire at health office, No. 12 Beacon Street.

The **Central Burying Ground**, on the Boylston Street side of the Common, is the least interesting of the ancient cemeteries of the town. It was laid out in 1756, but the oldest stone, with the exception of one which was removed from some other ground, is dated 1761. Stuart, the portrait-painter, was buried here, and Monsieur Julien, the inventor of the famous soup that bears his name. Julien's public house was for some years on the corner of Milk and Congress streets. He died in 1805, but his soup is still flourishing. It is supposed that several of the British soldiers who died from wounds received at Bunker Hill, or from disease in the barracks during the Siege, were buried here; but there is nothing to prove this, and the statement is questioned. Drake says that they were buried in a common trench, and that many of the remains were exhumed when changes in the northwest corner of the yard were made. This burying ground formerly extended to Boylston Street, and it was contracted to its present dimensions when the Boylston Street mall was laid out in 1839.

V.
THEATERS AND OTHER AMUSE-
MENTS.

Boston is known to the theatrical world as one of the best show towns in the country. This is the more remarkable, as it was many years after the play-house was flourishing in other cities before the Puritan City consented to its establishment in her midst. In 1750 an act was passed " to prevent stage plays and other theatrical enter-tainments," imposing heavy fines on the owner of the premises in which such entertainments should be given in defiance of the law, and upon the spectators and actors as well. Several unsuccessful attempts were made to secure the repeal of this act, during the years succeeding, before it finally disappeared from the statute books.

During the past few years, theaters have multiplied with marvel-ous rapidity. Twenty years ago, the Boston, the Globe, the Museum, the Howard, and a few cheap variety houses, were the only theaters in the city. To this list have since been added the Tremont, the Columbia, the Park, the Bowdoin Square, the Castle Square, and Keith's. Boston now has about fifteen theaters, properly so called, besides several places where similar entertainments are often given.

Alphabetical List of Theaters.

The Boston Museum, at 28 Tremont Street, between Court and School streets, is the oldest theater in the city. Its history dates back to 1841, and the present substantial granite structure has been occupied since 1846. The interior arrangements of the theater have been several times reconstructed and improvements made, and it is one of the best equipped play-houses of the day. It is noted for its production of new plays from foreign authors for the first time on the American stage, as well as for its magnificent revivals of the standard English comedies. The Museum maintained the stock system until 1893, and many famous actors and actresses have been, at different times, connected with its company. It has had uninterrupted success for over half a century, a record that can not be paralleled by the history of any other place of amusement in the United States.

It has a seating capacity of 1,500. Prices range from $1 to 35 cents, and some of the best seats in the house can be had for 50 cents.

Boston Theater, 539 Washington, between West and Avery streets. This theater was opened in 1854, and it was, for many years, the largest and most magnificent play-house in America. The exterior of the building is unpretentious, and almost buried from sight behind the adjacent buildings ; but within it is, in every respect, substantial and imposing. The lobbies are spacious, the staircases broad, and every convenience for the comfort of the audience is supplied. The auditorium is 90 feet in diameter, and reaches a height of 54 feet. The stage is 85 feet deep, and 66 feet high to the fly-floor. The curtain opening is 48 x 41 feet. The house seats 3,000 persons. There is a wide front entrance on Washington Street, and a rear one on Mason Street, and the means of egress are so ample that 1,000 persons can be dismissed in a minute. The prices range from $1.50 to 50 cents.

Bowdoin Square Theater. — This theater is located in Bowdoin Square, and was opened to the public in February, 1892. It has a broad, handsome lobby and auditorium decorated in old ivory and gold. The stage is large, and the proscenium opening is 36 feet wide by 32 feet high. It will seat 1,500 people, and the prices range from $1.50 to 25 cents.

The Castle Square Theater, opened in November, 1894, occupies the fortress-like building at 421 Tremont Street. This theater is absolutely fireproof, and, in comfort and beauty, it has no superior. Fronting on the square formed by the junction of Tremont, Ferdinand, and Chandler streets, with electric cars to all parts of the city and suburbs passing its door, it is one of the most accessible places of amusement in Boston. The stage combines every improvement at present known to the theatrical world. The space is ample, providing for 40 feet proscenium opening, 50 feet to back wall, 70 feet between walls, and 85 feet high, and, in addition, broad entrances on each side of the stage lead to the streets adjoining. A cavalcade of horses can enter at one side, make the circuit of the stage, and go out without that jostling which has spoiled so many stage pictures. The theater cost $1,500,000. It seats 1,700 people. Prices are popular, and a good seat can be had for 50 cents.

Chickering Hall, 151 Tremont Street, is used for concerts, lectures, and amateur dramatic entertainments.

The Columbia Theater occupies an entire block on Washington Street, and comprises the numbers from 978 to 986, inclusive. In design it follows the Moorish style, and its towers rise above the surrounding buildings. The interior finish and the furnishings are in harmony with the exterior architecture. The line of sight throughout the house is perfect, so that it matters not whether the spectator occupies the front row of the orchestra or a corner in the upper balcony, a complete view of the stage is had in either place. The Columbia will seat 1,600, and the prices range from $1.50 to 25 cents.

Grand Museum.—This is located on the corner of Washington and Dover streets. It is a variety theater with continuous performance from 1 to 10.30 P. M. Popular prices, 10 and 20 cents.

The Grand Opera House is at 1176 Washington Street, on the corner of Ashland Place. This is the chief South End theater, and performances are given by a stock company and by combinations. Prices range from $1 to 25 cents.

The Hollis Street Theater occupies the site of the old Hollis Street Church, at No. 10 Hollis Street. It was reconstructed from the church, and was opened November 9, 1885. It is one of the most thoroughly built edifices of its kind in the city, and it is especially well arranged in the particulars of safety from fire and means of quick and easy egress. It has a large auditorium, beautifully decorated and well lighted. The stage is spacious, and the pieces produced here are well mounted. The auditorium has a seating capacity of 1,600. The prices range from $1.50 to 25 cents.

The Howard Athenæum, 34 Howard Street, near Scollay Square, was first opened as a theater on the evening of October 13, 1845. During the following winter the theater was burned, but it was immediately rebuilt. In its early days it was the representative theater of the city. Since 1868 it has been a variety theater. It seats 1,500. Prices range from 10 to 25 cents. There is a continuous performance from 1 to 10 P. M.

Huntington Hall is in the Rogers Building of the Institute of

Technology. It is where the Lowell Institute lectures are given and is the place of meeting of the Society of Arts.

Horticultural Hall, an ornamental building of white granite, which stands on Tremont Street, between Bromfield and Bosworth streets, is the headquarters of the Massachusetts Horticultural Society, one of the oldest institutions of its kind in the country, dating from 1829. The exterior of the building is massive and elegant in proportion. The granite statues of Ceres, surmounting the central division of the façade, of Flora on the north buttress of the second story, and of Pomona on the south buttress, were executed by Martin Milmore. On the second and third floors, respectively, are the halls of the society, in which its exhibitions are given. These halls are also often let for various classes of entertainments and for fashionable balls. Portraits and busts of the founders, presidents, and benefactors of the society adorn the walls. The building was erected in 1864.

Keith's New Theater, 547 Washington Street, is the prettiest theater in Boston, and one of the prettiest in this country. It is a variety theater, with a continuous performance from 10.30 A. M. to 10.30 P. M. Even people who do not care for variety shows enjoy going to Keith's for the delight and exhilaration afforded by the gayest and most brilliant example of the rococo style in the city. "The lobby of this theater," says a recent writer, " is worthy of a French palace in the Louis XV period." Admission from 25 to 50 cents.

The Lyceum Theater is at 665 Washington Street, just south of Boylston. This is another variety theater, with continuous performance from 1 to 10.30 P. M. Popular prices from 10 to 50 cents.

Music Hall.—The main entrance to this hall is from Winter Street. This is a plain brick building, without architectural pretensions. It was built by private enterprise and opened in 1852. It is 130 feet long, 78 feet wide, and 65 feet high. Among the decorations are a fine statue of Apollo, various casts presented by Charlotte Cushman, and a magnificent statue of Beethoven, by Crawford, which stands on the platform. The last mentioned was presented by Charles C. Perkins. The acoustic properties of the hall are perfect, but the old Music Hall is a dreary, uncomfortable place, which has lost its handsome feature, the " big organ," and never can be made to look festive again. Here are given the grand oratorio performances of the Handel and Haydn Society, the Symphony concerts of the Harvard Musical Association, the concerts of the Boston Symphony Orchestra, the occasional concerts of the Apollo, Boylston, and other noted clubs. During the early summer season the popular promenade concerts are nightly given by a picked orchestra. These are conducted somewhat after the Continental fashion, with the accompaniments of beer, tobacco, Strauss waltzes, occasional groups of Harvard boys, and the foliage of prim little spruce-trees set about in tubs under the electric lights. They are locally designated " Pops."

Mechanics' Hall is in the magnificent building of the Massachusetts Charitable Mechanic Association, on Huntington Avenue, corner of West Newton Street. It was built especially for the public exhibitions (held about once in three years) of American manufactures and mechanic arts. [See MASSACHUSETTS CHARITABLE MECHANIC ASSOCIATION in Chapter VIII.] It contains sittings for 8,000 people, and is frequently let for grand opera and other large entertainments. It has all the conveniences for large gatherings and one of the finest organs in the country.

Museum (Austin & Stone's). -- This is a dime museum and variety theater, located at 4 Tremont Row. Continuous performance. Admission, 10 to 25 cents.

Palace Theater, 109 Court Street. This is another of the low-priced variety theaters, giving a continuous performance. Admission, 10 to 25 cents.

Park Theater.—This is a small theater, located at 117 Washington Street. It was constructed from the old Beethoven Hall and dates from 1879. It is a high-class combination house, and the names of many great actors and actresses are associated with its stage. Though the house is small, the space is so thoroughly utilized that seats are provided for over 1,100 people. The stage is spacious and well supplied with scenery and properties. Prices range from $1.50 to 50 cents.

Tremont Theater.— This is located at 176 Tremont Street. It was built for Henry E. Abbey and John B. Schoeffel. The auditorium is 75 feet high, of the same width, and 80 feet deep. It is fashioned on the plan of a mammoth shell. On the main floor there are no flat surfaces of any length. By this arrangement the hearing, as well as the sight, gains. The ten oddly-fashioned private boxes on either side of the proscenium give a novel effect to the interior. The decoration of the main ceiling is modernized Renaissance, treated in Gobelin-tapestry effect, and the coloring of the walls is in harmonizing shades. The stage is 73 by 45 feet, with a height of 69 feet to the rigging-loft. The house has 2,000 seats. The main entrance is exceptionally fine, and forms a broad vestibule, lobby, and foyer. Prices range from $1.50 to 50 cents.

The Turnhalle, at 29 Middlesex Street, is the headquarters of the Turners. It has a pretty little theater, in which German plays are occasionally given.

Tremont Temple, 82 Tremont Street, is a fine new building erected on the site of the old Temple, which was destroyed by fire in 1893. It will, when finished, be occupied on Sundays as a place of worship, and occasionally on the evenings of other days for concerts, lectures, etc.

Museums and Collections.

Boston Athenæum, 10 Beacon Street. There is a collection of valuable paintings and statuary in the grand vestibule and stair-case of the Athenæum Building, which can be seen by visitors on any week-day without charge. The library is a private one, and can be visited only upon the introduction of a member.

Boston Museum, 28 Tremont Street, between School and Court streets. This is a large collection of statuary, paintings, coins, etc. Open day and evening. Admission, 35 cents.

Barnum Museum.— Tuft's College, College Hill, Medford. This fine natural history collection was the gift of the late P. T. Barnum, the famous amusement manager, and is destined to become one of the most interesting museums in the United States, additions being frequently made to it. Among the unique features of the collection is the stuffed skin of the famous elephant, "Jumbo," and many other rare and curious specimens.

Bunker Hill Museum.—At the base of Bunker Hill Monument, Charlestown District, there is kept a collection of interesting Colonial and Revolutionary relics,

Botanical Garden, Cambridge. This is one of the largest and finest collections of plants and flowers in the country. Open to the public.

The Boston Natural History Museum is in the building of the Natural History Society, corner of Boylston and Berkeley streets, and it is maintained by this society. The collection of stuffed mammals, birds, fishes, shells, minerals, and other specimens here exhibited is one of the most valuable in the country. It is free to the public for several hours on Wednesdays and Saturdays. A guide meets visitors in the vestibule at 10 and 11 A. M. on those days. On other days it is open from 10 to 5 o'clock, and an admission fee of 25 cents is charged.

Faneuil Hall Collection of Historical Paintings. — Merchants' Row and Faneuil Hall Square. The thousands who visit this shrine of American patriotism will find an interesting collection of historical paintings and portraits. It is open to visitors every day (except Sunday) from 9 A. M. to 4 P. M. [See " Faneuil Hall," in Chapter IV.]

Historic Genealogical Collection, 18 Somerset Street. At the rooms of the New England Historic Genealogical Society may be seen a large and valuable collection of old engravings, prints, and books, possessing great interest for historians, genealogists, antiquarians, and all who are interested in the genealogies of New England. The rooms are open to the public, without charge, every week-day from 9 A. M. to 5 P. M. except Saturdays, when the hours are from 9 A. M. to 1 P. M.

Krino Grotto, Museum, and Gardens, Wellesley. William Emerson Baker, a few years since, converted his noted Ridge Hill Farms into one of the most unique pleasure-grounds. There are rare and beautiful plants, a zoölogical collection, aquarium, underground gardens and ferneries, grottoes, and various other novel features. A nominal admission fee is charged.

Massachusetts Historical Museum, No. 30 Tremont Street. The Massachusetts Historical Society has here a rare collection of curiosities. Among them are the swords of Sir William Pepperell, Miles Standish, Colonel Prescott, and others ; a phial of the tea washed ashore after its having been thrown into the harbor at the " Boston tea party "; an oak chair brought over in " The Mayflower "; the diary of Judge Samuel Sewall ; King Philip's samp-bowl; portraits of Governors Winthrop, Endicott, and Winslow, and many other objects of interest. Open from 9 A. M. to 5 P. M. Admission free.

Museum (Agassiz) of Comparative Zoology, Oxford Street, Cambridge. This great museum, which has no equal in America, was founded under the direction of Louis Agassiz, one of the foremost naturalists of the world, who was associated with its direction until his death. The exhibition rooms comprise the synoptic rooms, the rooms containing the collections of mammals, birds, reptiles, fishes, mollusks, crustacea, insects, radiates, sponges, protozoa, faunal collections of North and South America, the Indo-Asiatic, the African, and other realms. Here, also, is a collection of glass flowers, a most wonderful display of imitations of flowers, made by Leopold and Rudolph Blaschka of Germany, to whom alone the process of making and coloring is known. The museum belongs to Harvard University. Open to visitors, every week-day throughout the year, from 9 to 5.

The Old South Museum.—In the Old South Church, corner of Washington and Milk streets, is quite a valuable collection of Revolutionary and historical relics. The museum is open on week-days from 9 A. M. to 6 P. M. Admission, 25 cents. [See Old South Meeting-House, in Chapter IV.]

Old State House Collection, Washington, corner of State Street. The upper portion of the Old State House is now utilized for exhibition rooms of relics of historical interest, under the control of the Bostonian Society. Paintings, portraits, antiquities, etc., form a very interesting collection which every visitor should see. Open to the public every day, except Sunday, from 9.30 A. M. to 5.30 P. M. Admission free.

Peabody Museum of American Archæology and Ethnology, Cambridge. This was founded by George Peabody, who gave, in all, $150,000 ; of this sum, $60,000 were reserved for a building, which was finished in 1877. The museum preserves implements and ornaments relating to the aboriginal races.

In July, 1891, the government of Honduras gave to the museum, by a special edict, the charge of the antiquities of that country for ten years, with the privilege of bringing to the museum one-half of the collection obtained by explorations of the ancient cities and burial places within the borders of the country. The Serpent Mound Park, in Adams County, Ohio, containing the great Serpent Mound, is the property of the Peabody Museum. Open to the public every week-day from 9 to 5 o'clock. Admission free.

The Warren Museum of Natural History is at 82 Chestnut Street. This is a private museum, formed, principally, from collections made by Dr. J. C. Warren, the noted surgeon. Among the curious objects on exhibition are the skeleton of the mastodon (the only perfect skeleton of the kind anywhere), and many other skeletons ; casts from various objects in the British Museum, mummies,

7

casts of eggs of mammoth birds, and many other objects of great
interest. The collection is preserved in a fireproof building erected
for the purpose. There is no charge for admission.

The State House Collection, Beacon Street, head of Park Street.
One can pass an interesting and profitable hour or two in looking at
the many historical memorials exhibited here. The collection of
stones, statues, busts, tablets, battle-flags, cannon, etc., is rare and
valuable. Admission free.

Music and Musical Societies.

The atmosphere of Boston is full of music, and it is the most assid-
uously cultivated of all the arts. The regular weekly concerts of the
Symphony Orchestra, with the still more popular "rehearsals," draw
enthusiastic audiences from early in the autumn until late in the
spring. The opera seasons are brief and more or less uncertain;
but Boston makes the most of what she can get and hopes for better
times. A recent writer says that if "a stranger wished to get a
glimpse of a typical old-time Bostonese crowd he could do no better
than to attend a Christmas oratorio by the Handel and Haydn Society
in the Music Hall, and, without flippancy, it may be said that he
would hear heavenly music sung as well as it is likely to be sung here
below. An eminent musical critic has made the remark that if
there were three of him he might make himself 'go around' so as to
cover the concerts that are given in the season, and this conveys but
a hint of the wonderful activity in the musical life of the community."
The following is a list of the principal musical societies of the city:

Alphabetical List of Musical Societies.

The Apollo Club was formed in 1871, by a few leading singers in
church choirs in the city, for the performance of part-songs and cho-
ruses for male voices. The number of active members varies from
sixty to eighty. The number of associate members is limited to 500.
The associate members, for an annual assessment, receive tickets to
all the concerts given by the club. Its membership has included the
best vocalists of Boston among the active members, and the success
of the club has been such that similar clubs have been formed in
many other cities, some of them taking the same name. No public
concerts are given, and no tickets to its performances are sold. It has
convenient club-rooms and a hall for its weekly rehearsals. Its concerts are generally given in Music Hall.

The Boylston Club is a private musical society, which was organized in 1872, for the study of music for male voices only. In 1876 the club was enlarged by the formation of an auxiliary chorus for ladies. It gives cantatas, masses, psalms, and four-part songs of the great composers, and leaves oratorios to the Handel and Haydn Society. The active membership now numbers nearly 200. The rehearsals are given in the Mechanics' Hall, in the building of the Massachusetts Charitable Mechanics' Association, and its concerts in Music Hall. Admission is by tickets, obtainable only from members of the club.

The Boston Symphony Orchestra is a permanent organization, established through the liberality of Mr. Henry Lee Higginson. During the season it gives weekly concerts in Music Hall. It is doing a great deal toward educating the people in classical music.

The Cecilia Society was originally formed in 1874, within the Harvard Musical Association, for part-singing for mixed voices. Until 1876 the Cecilia took part in Harvard Symphony concerts only; but in that year it was reorganized and established on a new and independent basis, with 125 active members. Later associate members were added, the limit being fixed at 250, who bear the expenses of the association, receiving tickets to the concerts, of which four are given in each season. Admission to the concerts is secured only by membership or by invitation of members.

The Orpheus Musical Society dates from 1853. It is the leading musical association among the Germans of Boston. At first only Germans were admitted to membership, then Americans were permitted to become associate members, and now, for several years, they have been welcomed to full membership. The Orpheus is a social as well as a musical club, and its rooms are the scene of many a pleasant festival. During each season it gives several concerts.

The Harvard Musical Association was organized in 1837, to "promote progress and knowledge of the best music," and it has done much toward fulfilling its mission. It has a valuable library of music, and works of history, theory, and general musical literature, open to members only.

The Handel and Haydn Society.—This association, with a single exception, is the oldest musical society in the country—the oldest being the Stoughton Musical Society, formed in 1786. The Handel and Haydn was established in 1815, originating in a meeting to which were invited all who were interested in "the subject of cultivating and improving a correct taste in the performance of sacred music." Its first oratorio was given in King's Chapel, on Christmas Eve of 1815, with a chorus of 100 voices, only ten of them being female voices. Its orchestra then consisted of less than a dozen performers and an organ accompaniment. From that time to the present the society has kept up its efforts to cultivate a popular taste for the best music. It has a membership of about 500. Its concerts are given in the Music Hall.

Athletics.

There are several private gymnasiums in Boston, two of the best of which are the *Allen Gymnasium for Women and Children*, and the *Posse Gymnasium*, for both men and women. The former was founded in 1878 by Miss Mary E. Allen. It consists of a school for body training (the course covering six years), and a college of gymnastics for the education of teachers. The school is provided with bowling alleys, and tennis courts, and with Turkish baths. The Posse Gymnasium, at 23 Irvington Street, was established in 1890, and includes a normal school for gymnastic training. It is fitted with Swedish and other apparatus. Fencing is among the branches taught.

The *Young Men's Christian Association*, at 458 Boylston Street; the *Young Men's Christian Union*, 48 Boylston Street, and the *Young Women's Christian Association*, 40 Berkeley Street, all have large and finely equipped gymnasiums.

The **Boston Athletic Association** is one of the largest organizations of its class in the country. It occupies a fine club-house on Exeter Street, corner of Blagden, which is one of the best equipped of its kind in the country. It has tennis, racquet, and hand-ball courts, fencing and boxing rooms, billiard-rooms, bowling alleys, Turkish bath, and swimming tank, and a great gymnasium provided with the most approved apparatus. There are also all the regular features of a modern club, including a large restaurant and supper-rooms. The club was organized in 1888, and has over 2,000 members.

Field Sports.

Boston is an enthusiastic patron of field sports which are designed as games for pleasure rather than exercise in strength and skill.

Baseball is played in Boston every day during the season, and there are any number of clubs devoted to this sport.

The *Boston Baseball Grounds* are off Walpole Street, Tremont Street, South End. The day and hour of all games are abundantly advertised.

Other Clubs.—There are numberless *Fencing*, *Cricket*, *Bicycle*, *Racquet*, *Tennis*, *Yachting*, *Rowing*, and kindred clubs, many having fine club-houses, and information concerning them is easily obtained.

Lectures in Boston are frequent, and the advertisements in the daily papers, especially *The Transcript*, *The Globe*, and *The Herald*, should be scrutinized for information by any one interested. Chickering and Huntington halls, and the halls of the Y. M. C. A., the Y. M. C. U., and the Y. W. C. A., are the usual places for their delivery. The LOWELL INSTITUTE LECTURES, which are a permanent feature of educational work, are intended to promote the moral, intellectual, and physical instruction and education of the inhabitants. Tickets may be obtained as advertised in the newspapers. Technical lectures on mechanics are given every year at the Wells Memorial Institute, 987 Washington Street. The details of the courses are announced in October. The Y. M. C. A., the Y. M. C. U., the Y. W. C. A., and the Woman's Educational and Industrial Union, give courses of lectures at stated times during the year.

VI.
EDUCATIONAL INSTITUTIONS, LIBRARIES, ETC.

Public Schools.

In 1635, less than five years after the settlement of Boston, a free school was opened for "the teaching and nourishing of children," and thus Boston is entitled to the honor of laying the foundation of the free-school system of America. Boston may well point with pride to her public schools, which, according to recent statistics, comprise 603 general and special schools, with a registration of 72,104, an average daily attendance of 56,364, and nearly 1,500 teachers. Among the special schools are the Horace Mann School for Deaf Mutes, and a number of evening schools for the teaching of elementary and classical branches and drawing.

The Boys' Latin and English High School will interest visitors more than any of the other public schools, because of its traditions and the many eminent men who have been among its pupils and graduates. It occupies the block bounded by Dartmouth, Montgomery, and Clarendon streets and Warren Avenue. The entrance to the Latin School is on the Warren Avenue front, and that to the English High School on the Montgomery Street side. The structure is of brick, with sandstone trimmings. Most of the exterior ornamentation consists of terra-cotta heads in the gables of the dormer windows, and terra-cotta frieze courses, the work of S. H. Bartlett, the sculptor. Both the main vestibules are decorated with statuary. On the Latin School side is the marble monument, by Richard S. Greenough, dedicated to those graduates of the school who took part in the Civil War. On the

English High School side is a marble group, by Benzoni, of the
" Flight from Pompeii," the gift of Henry P. Kidder, who was a
graduate of the school. William P. Clough was the architect of
the building, which was dedicated February 22, 1881. The *Latin
School* is the oldest school in the country, antedating Harvard by
nearly two years. Its first school-house stood on ground now
covered, in part, by King's Chapel, and gave School Street its
name. Among the honored names enrolled as pupils at different
periods in its history, we find those of Benjamin Franklin, John
Hancock, Samuel Adams, Robert Treat Paine, William Hooper,
Charles Sumner, Ralph Waldo Emerson, Rt. Rev. John B.
Fitzpatrick, Revs. Cotton Mather, Henry Ward Beecher, Edward
Everett Hale, and Bishop Phillips Brooks. The *English High
School* was opened in May, 1821, to meet a want which was ex-
pressed in the report of a committee appointed to consider the
feasibility of establishing an English classical school. " The mode
of education now adopted," ran the report, " and the branches of
knowledge that are taught at our English grammar schools, are
not sufficiently extensive, nor otherwise calculated to bring the
powers of the mind into operation, nor to qualifying a youth to
fill, usefully and respectably, many of those stations, both public
and private, in which he may be placed. A parent who wishes to
give a child an education that shall fit him for active life, and
shall serve as a foundation for eminence in his profession, whether
mercantile or mechanical, is under the necessity of giving him a
different education from any which our public schools can now
furnish. Hence, many children are separated from their parents
and sent to private academies in this vicinity to acquire that
instruction which can not be obtained at the public seminaries."
The school more than fulfilled the hopes of its projectors, and is
to-day one of the " model " schools of the United States.

The Girls' Latin and High School Building is on the corner of
West Newton and Pembroke streets. It has a front on each one of
these streets of 144 feet, and a depth of 131 feet. The *Girls' High School*
was established in 1855, in connection with the Normal School. In 1872
the two were separated. The *Girls' Latin School* was established
in 1878, to provide a training for girls similar to that given the boys
at the old Latin School. The building is well ventilated and roomy,
and every facility is afforded for thorough work in the different

departments. A large collection of casts of sculpture and statuary, the gifts of admiring friends, is in the hall of the upper story. On the roof is an octagonal structure designed for use as an astronomical observatory.

Among the **Grammar Schools** which are especially worthy of notice are the *Dwight*, the *Everett*, and the *Prince*. The last named was the first school-house in New England arranged on the German and Austrian plan. By this plan the rooms on each floor are placed on one side of a long corridor, instead of around a common hall in the middle. Among the advantages claimed for this method of construction are better ventilation, better light, and a more direct connection between the corridors and street entrances.

The Horace Mann School for Deaf Mutes is on the east side of Newbury Street, next to the South Congregational Church, which stands at the corner of Exeter Street. It is in an attractive building of face-brick and block free-stone façade, with a high-arched entrance-way. The pupils are here taught to communicate by articulation rather than by signs. They are also trained in Sloyd carving, in drawing and penmanship, and other useful arts.

The Boston Normal School is in the third story of the Rice School Building, on Dartmouth Street. It was established in the city of Boston in 1852, by the city council, on the recommendation of the school committee. It is interesting to note the ground on which this action was based. In the language of a member of the school committee : '' The friends for further opportunities for the graduates of our girls' grammar schools," fearing to revive an old controversy, hesitated to move for a high school ; and, therefore, in the faith that they should find no opposition to the preparation of female teachers, established a normal school.

'' It was found, however, that girls fresh from the grammar schools were not fit candidates for normal training." So, in 1854, the school committee, with the view of adapting the school to the double purpose of giving its pupils high school and normal instruction, caused '' the introduction of a few additional branches of study, and a slight alteration in the arrangement of the course," and called it the Girls' High and Normal School. But the normal features were soon quite overshadowed by the high school work.

To remedy this defect, a training department was organized in 1864, and located in Somerset Street ; but in 1870 this department was transferred to the then new building, on West Newton Street, occupied by the Girls' High and Normal School.

The school was continued under the double name of Girls' High and Normal School till 1872. At this time the school committee, finding that the normal element had again been crowded out by the high school work, and that the school had almost lost its distinctively professional character, " separated the two courses, and returned the normal school to its original condition, as a separate school. Since then its work has been " giving professional instruction to young women who intend to become teachers in the public schools of Boston."

Boston University.—This institution, for the liberal education of both sexes, was incorporated in 1869 by Lee Claflin, Isaac Rich, and Jacob Sleeper. Its headquarters are in Jacob Sleeper Hall, on Somerset Street, near Beacon. It embraces three colleges, three professional schools, and a post-graduate department of universal science. In Jacob Sleeper Hall are the College of Liberal Arts and the School of All Sciences; near at hand, in Ashburton Place, is the Law School Building; at 72 Mount Vernon Street is the Theological School (Methodist), and the School of Medicine, connected with the Massachusetts Homœopathic Hospital, is at the south end. The College of Music was, in 1891, adopted by the New England Conservatory of Music, and constitutes the graduate department of that institution. The College of Agriculture was established in 1875 by an agreement with the Massachusetts Agricultural College at Amherst. The School of Law was the first in this country to present a three-years' course of study. The School of Medicine was also the first to establish a four-years' course of instruction, and which, at the end of three-year courses, confers the degree of Bachelor of Medicine or Bachelor of Surgery. Most of the faculty of the School of Medicine are homœopathic in theory, but its statutes provide for the coöperation of any incorpted State medical society in the United States in the testing and graduation of students. The School of All Sciences was organized in 1874, and it is open to graduates only. It is designed, first, for the benefit of bachelors of arts, philosophy, or science, of whatsoever college, who may desire to receive post-graduate instruction; and, secondly, to meet the wants of graduates in law, theology, medicine, or other professional courses, who may wish to supplement their studies with higher education. It has about twelve hundred matriculated students, nearly one-third of whom are women.

Boston College, on Harrison Avenue, adjoining the Church of the Immaculate Conception, was founded, in 1860, by the Fathers of the Society of Jesus, and it is conducted by that organization. It has power to confer all degrees usually conferred by colleges, except medical. It presents a long and thorough course of instruction, in which classical studies occupy a prominent place. It enrolls about 400 students, and has a corps of nineteen or twenty professors. The college buildings are plain brick structures, covering quite a large area.

Chauncy Hall School, on Boylston, between Clarendon and Dartmouth streets, is the oldest private school in Boston, having been founded in 1828. It was first established in Chauncy Street, from which circumstance it gained its name. It is for both sexes, and carries the pupil from the kindergarten, through all the departments, to the college preparatory. It was the first school in Boston to adopt the military drill. The building has an attractive exterior, and its interior is arranged with careful regard to sanitary conditions and the convenience of teachers and pupils.

Harvard University.— On October 28, 1636, the General Court of Massachusetts Bay voted "to give £400 towards a schoole or colledge." This sum represented an amount equal to the whole years' tax of the entire colony. In 1637 the college was ordered established at Newton, and the name was changed to Cambridge. In this same year Nathaniel Eaton was appointed master of the school, and under his superintendence a small wooden house was built near the site of the present Wadsworth House. It had about an acre of land around it and some thirty apple trees. Eaton proved to be a harsh and penurious manager, and the scholars rebelled at the bad food. As a result, Eaton was discharged. In 1638, the institution received the liberal bequest of about £780, and also 260 books, from the Rev. John Harvard, late of Emmanuel College, Cambridge, England, who died at Charlestown in that year. The General Court, in memory of the noble benefactor, gave the college his name. The college was thus placed on a secure financial foundation, which has been strengthened and maintained by good management and the generosity of the alumni and other friends. Though connected with Colonial and State governments, the university has been from the first a private rather than a public institution, supported, in the main, by the fees paid by its students and the income from permanent funds from time to time given it by friends of education.

MEMORIAL HALL, HARVARD COLLEGE — Cambridge.

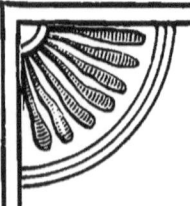

F·H·JOHNSON·&·Co.

Wholesale
Retail
and
Commission Dealers
in all kinds of

...FRESH FISH

Stall 114...Faneuil Hall Market,

· BOSTON ·

Harvard is not only the oldest, but one of the richest, of American colleges. She possesses property worth $12,000,000 ; her roll of graduates, living and dead, contains nearly 20,000 names ; and, in round numbers, her 3,000 students are taught by 300 professors and instructors. Her list of eminent sons comprises the names of John Adams, John Quincy Adams, W. E. Channing, Edward Everett, W. H. Prescott, George Bancroft, Ralph Waldo Emerson, Oliver Wendell Holmes, Charles Sumner, John Lothrop Motley, James Russell Lowell, E. E. Hale, and Henry D. Thoreau.

In Cambridge, Harvard has the college, the graduate school, the Divinity school, the Lawrence scientific school, and the law school ; in Boston proper are the dental school, the medical school, and the school of veterinary medicine ; and in Jamaica Plain are the Bussey Institution and the Arnold Arboretum. Each of these departments is endowed with its own funds, and independent of all others, except that all are under one management. The scientific departments include the astronomical observatory, laboratories of chemistry, physics, natural history, psychology, and physiology ; museums of comparative zoölogy, botany, geology, mineralogy, and archæology ; botanic gardens, and herbaria. The university museum has four acres of floor space, and the collections of the museum of comparative zoölogy alone cost $350,000.

The *College Yard* is entered by a gateway built of granite, brick, sandstone, and iron. It was erected with funds left by Mr. Samuel Johnson of the class of 1855. On its panels are carved the shields of the State, city, and college, an emblem to the donor and the nation, and quotations from the early college history and Colonial records. The Yard contains about twenty-two acres, and nearly all the available space is occupied by the buildings necessary to an institution of such magnitude. *Massachusetts Hall* is the most ancient structure about the Yard ; it was built in 1820. *Harvard Hall* dates from 1766. Then, there are *University Hall*, *Gore Hall*, containing the University Library; the *Boylston Chemical Laboratory*, *Sever Hall*, *Holden Chapel*, *Appleton Chapel*, *Mathews Hall*, *Grays Hall*, *Weld Hall*, etc., all in the Yard.

To the northward the university has encroached on the old playgrounds, Holmes and Jarvis fields, and is rapidly spreading all over that part of Cambridge, with its vast group of halls, laboratories, museums, gymnasiums, and professional schools, its botanical gardens and observatory, forming a small city in themselves. Some of the recently erected dormitories are fine specimens of architecture, and deserve special notice. Among these are *Thayer Hall*, containing sixty-eight suites of rooms, built in 1870, at a cost of $115,000, by Nathaniel Thayer, of a wealthy Boston family, in memory of his father, a minister of the same name, and of his brother, John Eliot Thayer; *Grays Hall*, erected in 1863, commemorating the generous gifts of the well-known Gray family of Boston; *Mathews Hall*, a Gothic brick building, erected in 1870, containing sixty suites of rooms, and *Hastings Hall*, one of the finest of the college dormitories, built in 1890, costing $243,000, the bequest of Walter Hastings.

Memorial Hall, architecturally the most imposing of the university buildings, was erected by the alumni, in 1870-77, as a memorial to the Harvard men who died in the Civil War. The building is of brick and sandstone, 310 feet long and 115 feet wide. The central division is the solemn Memorial Transept, lined with marble tablets, set in black walnut screens, bearing the names of the fallen heroes, and the places and times of their deaths. The transept is 115 feet long and 58 feet high to the handsome vaulted roof. Over this transept a sturdy tower rises to the height of 200 feet, and forms a conspicuous landmark. The huge Gothic dining-hall, seating 1,000 students, opens from the transept. It is 164 feet long, 60 feet wide, and 80 feet high to its timber roof, with galleries at either end, and at the west end an immense stained-glass window, with the arms of the Republic, the State, and the university. The walls are adorned with fine old portraits and busts, the works of Copley, Stuart, Trumbull, Hunt, Harding, Powers, Crawford, Story, Greenough, and other eminent artists. Directly opposite this hall, on the right of the transept, is the entrance to Sanders' Theater, a semi-circular hall, with graded seats, accommodating 1,500 persons. This is where class-day and graduation exercises are held. The story of the founding of Harvard College is told in the Latin inscriptions over the stage. The wall back of the stage is ornamented with the college seal, three books bearing the word "*Veritas*" (truth). Josiah Quincy, a statue of whom in marble, by Story, stands near the stage, was the sixteenth president of the college. He was born in Boston in 1772, of a famous family, which gave its name to John Quincy Adams and to the town of Quincy, and is still represented by the same old-fashioned baptismal name. He was for eight years in Congress, for six years mayor

LAW LIBRARY, HARVARD COLLEGE — Cambridge.

Old Fashioned Marshmallows

W. G. FIELD. E. H. TENEYCK.

Persian
Marshmallow
Company

**171 & 173 Wooster Street,
NEW YORK.**

NEAR BLEECKER STREET.

BLUE LABEL BRAND

RED LABEL BRAND

GOLD LABEL BRAND

of Boston — known as the "Great Mayor" — and for sixteen years president of Harvard. He wrote a history of the college, and last appeared at a meeting of the alumni in 1863, at the age of ninety-two.

The *statue of John Harvard*, which stands on "The Delta," was designed by Daniel G. French of Concord. It was given to the university by Samuel J. Bridge. There is no likeness of John Harvard in existence; but this statue, representing a young Puritan scholar, is emblematic of the courage and manhood of the founders of New England.

Libraries.—In addition to the various society libraries, the university has twenty-nine minor libraries connected with the various departments, containing nearly 100,000 volumes, while the University Library has over 350,000 volumes and 300,000 pamphlets. There are but two libraries in America larger than this one, the Public Library of Boston and the Congressional Library. The privileges of the library are extended to men of letters outside of the university jurisdiction.

The Annex is on the southeast corner of Garden and Mason streets. The main building is known as Fay House. This is the institution of the "Society for the Collegiate Instruction of Women," established in 1879 by Mr. Arthur Gilman. It has for its object the obtaining for women the best instruction given in Harvard. At the opening of the Annex there were twenty-seven women instructed by Harvard professors, forty of whom offered their services. The students come from all parts of the country ; from the Pacific coast and Sandwich Islands. They board in the various Cambridge homes, and recite at Fay House. The entrance examinations are the same as those at Harvard, and the certificates given to the graduates state that the holders have performed the work required by Harvard College for its B. A. degree. The certificates are awarded upon the recommendations of an academic board, composed almost exclusively of Harvard professors. *Fay House* contains recitation rooms, a reference library, and the botanical laboratory. In other buildings are laboratories of chemistry, physics, and biology. The collections of the college library and museums are open to the students, and opportunities for study in the Botanic Garden and Herbarium and the Astronomical Observatory are afforded.

Departments of Harvard Outside of Cambridge.

The Bussey Institution is a school of agriculture, horticulture, and veterinary science. Its grounds and buildings are in the

Jamaica Plain District of the city, near Forest Hills Station of the Providence division of the New York, New Haven & Hartford Railroad. They occupy a part of the noble estate bequeathed to the university by Benjamin Bussey, who also left funds in trust for the school. The Institute was opened in 1870. The building is a tasteful structure, in the Victoria Gothic architecture, of Roxbury pudding-stone, 112 feet long and 73 feet wide. (See Arnold Arboretum, Chapter III.)

The Harvard Dental School is located on North Grove Street, in a building formerly occupied by the Harvard Medical School.

The Harvard Medical School occupies the magnificent building on the southeast corner of Boylston and Exeter streets. This school was established at Cambridge, in the old Holden Chapel, in 1783. It was removed to Boston in 1810. The present building, completed in 1883, is of brick and red sandstone, four stories in height. The features of its broad front, which faces Boylston Street, are the three pavilions, and the sky-line of stone balustrades, and low gables surrounding the flat roof. The interior is admirably arranged. The spacious class-rooms, lecture-rooms, and laboratories are thoroughly equipped. On the third floor is the Museum of Comparative Anatomy, founded in 1846. The original collection of this museum was given by Dr. John Collins Warren, professor of anatomy and surgery in the school from 1815 to 1847. The full course at this school is four years, but on the completion of three years' study, and satisfactory examinations, the degree of Doctor of Medicine is conferred. The school numbers about 500 students, and has a corps of seventy-five professors, instructors, and assistants. The standard of the school is one of the highest in the country.

The School of Veterinary Medicine is on Village and Lucas streets. Besides the school building, there is a hospital, and at the Bussey Farm there are pastures and buildings pertaining to the school.

Other Institutions.

The Massachusetts Institute of Technology.— This, the leading technical school in this country, is located on Boylston Street, between Berkeley and Clarendon. It was founded in 1861, and its development has been broad and rapid. Its prominent feature is the

MASSACHUSETTS INSTITUTE OF TECHNOLOGY—Berkeley and Clarendon Streets.

School of Industrial Science, devoted to the teaching of science as applied to the various engineering professions — civil, mechanical, mining, electrical, chemical, and sanitary engineering — as well as to architecture, chemistry, metallurgy, physics, and geology. Courses of a less technical nature, designed as a preparation for business callings, and in biology, preparatory to the professional study of medicine, are also given; and the Lowell School of Practical Design is maintained by the corporation. The main building of the Institute of Technology, known as the *Rogers Building*, is the oldest and most attractive of the buildings, and contains over fifty rooms, most of them being laboratories or lecture-rooms. This building was named in honor of Prof. William B. Rogers, the first president, and one of the founders of the school. Here are the principal offices of the school. The *Walker Building*, next beyond, toward Clarendon Street, erected in 1884, is devoted, mainly, to the departments of physics, chemistry, and electricity. Other buildings are the *Architectural Building* and the *Engineering Building*, on Trinity Place; the *Workshops*, on Garrison Street, with a section devoted to the Lowell School of Design, and the *Gymnasium and Drill Hall* on Exeter Street.

The Massachusetts College of Pharmacy. — The College of Pharmacy is on the corner of St. Botolph and Garrison streets. It was instituted in 1823 and chartered in 1852. Women are admitted to this institution on the same conditions as men. Graduates receive the degree of Ph. G. The college building was erected in 1866, and is well arranged, with large lecture halls and laboratories, cabinets of botanical and chemical drugs, and a great herbarium. The Shepard Library is a valuable collection of pharmaceutical, chemical, and botanical works, the nucleus of which was the gift of Dr. A. B. Shepard. The college is under the direction of a board of trustees, and it has ten professors and instructors.

The New England Conservatory of Music, on Newton Street, facing Franklin Square, was established in 1867 by the late Dr. Eben Tourgee, and incorporated in 1870. The Conservatory embraces sixteen separate schools, with a college of music for advanced students, which is connected with Boston University. The building was originally the St. James Hotel, and it was acquired by the institution in 1882. It has a large concert hall, recitation and practice rooms, library and reading-rooms, parlors, museum, and quarters for many of the pupils, who board in the establishment. At the rear is Sleeper Hall, erected in 1885. The Conservatory is under the control of a board of trustees. The instructors number about 100, while the number of students is over 1,500.

The Normal Art School is on the southeast corner of Exeter and Newbury streets. It is under the direction of the State Board of Education, and was established in 1873, primarily as a training-school for teachers of industrial drawing in the public schools, but other students in special branches are admitted. In this building are class and lecture rooms for instruction in architectural and mechanical drawing and modeling in clay, in painting in oil and water-colors, and in other branches. The school is well equipped in every way. It has a museum and exhibition hall.

The Perkins Institution and Massachusetts School for the Blind is on East Broadway, South Boston. It is a semi-public institution, organized, in 1831, by the late Dr. Samuel G. Howe. Beginning with six blind children as the nucleus of the school, Doctor Howe continued as its director until his death, in 1877. Much of the success of the school is ascribed to his devotion to it, and his eminent fitness for the work. He was succeeded by his son-in-law, Dr. Michael Anagnos, who was for many years his faithful co-worker, and who established the kindergarten in the West Roxbury District (corner of Perkins and Day streets). The pupils use, in reading, the system of raised letters invented by Doctor Howe. The library, containing 11,000 volumes in raised type, is the largest general library for the blind in the world. The asylum also possesses an interesting museum and a complete gymnasium. Thirty practice-rooms are provided for piano pupils, and there is a large hall for the band and the special musical library. The institution is partly self-supporting, such of the pupils as are able to pay maintaining themselves at a boarding-school. All the pupils are taught some useful trade or profession. Several of the States pay for a large number of beneficiaries. In the arrangement of the establishment the family system is followed, and the girls occupy dwelling-houses by themselves, the sexes being separated. It is named the Perkins Institution, in honor of Col. Thomas W. Perkins, a Bostonian in his day distinguished for good deeds, and one of the most generous benefactors of the institution.

The Protestant Episcopal Theological School in Cambridge was founded, in 1867, on an endowment from Benjamin T. Reed of Boston.

It has eight professors and one instructor, and the number of students averages about forty. The stone buildings form a noble and harmonious group, including Lawrence Hall and Winthrop Hall, the dormitories, Reed Hall, a cloistered Gothic building, named after the founder, and which contains the library and lecture-rooms; and St. John's Memorial Chapel, built in 1869 by Robert Means Mason of Boston, as a memorial of his wife and brother, the Rev. Charles Mason, D. D. The chapel is a beautiful cruciform edifice of Roxbury granite and free-stone. Burnham Hall, behind the chapel, built in 1879 by the late John A. Burnham, contains a dining-room to accommodate over 100 students. Rev. George Zabriskie Gray, D. D., and Rev. Elisha Mulford, D. D., author of " The Nation " and " The Republic of God," were connected with this institution before their deaths. The library of Harvard University is open to members of the school.

St. John's Boston Ecclesiastical Seminary occupies a beautiful estate on Lake Street, in the Brighton District. This is a Roman Catholic institution, founded in 1880. It numbers ten professors and instructors and over 100 pupils.

Wellesley College is situated in the beautiful village of Wellesley, about fifteen miles from Boston, on Lake Waban. It has the largest and handsomest building in the world devoted exclusively to the higher education of women. The grounds comprise over 300 acres and are very beautiful.

Private Schools.—Besides the schools mentioned in the foregoing pages, Boston numbers about 100 private schools, which will compare favorably with those of any city in the country. About 5,000 pupils receive instruction in free denominational schools, which are chiefly Roman Catholic institutions.

Libraries.

The public and private libraries of Boston are in keeping with her other educational institutions. To her belongs the glory of possessing the largest public library for free circulation in the world, and this library is housed in the most magnificent public building in the country. Her many special libraries — law, medical, scientific, musical, and art — are superior to similar collections in other cities ; and the library of Harvard University, which has been mentioned elsewhere in this chapter, stands at the head of the great college libraries in the United States.

The Boston Public Library, on Dartmouth and Boylston streets, facing Copley Square, was first opened to the public with a nucleus of less than 10,000 books. It occupied quarters on Mason Street, and in 1858, moved into a building of its own on Boylston Street, opposite the Common. In February, 1895, it was moved to the new Public Library Building—" Built by the people and dedicated to the advancement of learning."

By successive annexations to the territory of the city, the libraries of the several cities and towns annexed have become branches of the Public Library, and are carried on as such. It has also received many bequests in money and books. The enumeration of all the books in the library on December 1, 1894, was 608,466. The library contains several special collections which add to the reputation of the institution, and make it a Mecca for scholars throughout the country. At present, these special libraries are eleven in number. The Patent Collection numbers nearly 5,000 volumes, and is open to indefinite growth. The Bowditch Mathematical Library, of nearly 6,000 volumes, is enlarged by the yearly income of a fund of $10,000. The Parker Library, of 14,000 volumes, was left by Theodore Parker, with the provision that they should be made as accessible as possible. The Prince Library, of about 3,000 volumes, is the most significant, if not the largest or most valuable, of all public collections of Americana in existence. The Barton Library, of nearly 14,000 volumes, contains many fine specimens of book-work and binding, as well as a remarkable Shakesperian collection. The Thayer Library, of more than 5,000 volumes, is interesting for its portraits and plates of historical and literary importance. The Franklin Library, of 500 volumes, was formed in memory of the great Bostonian, and is aided in part by the income of a gift from Dr. Samuel A. Green, who conceived the idea of making this memorial. The 600 choice volumes from the library of the late John A. Lewis are devoted to early and rare Americana. The Ticknor Library, of 6,000 volumes, is one of the finest collections of Spanish and Portuguese literature outside of Spain. The late George Ticknor left $4,000, the income of which is devoted to keeping up the high reputation of this collection. The trustees have recently been notified that they are to receive, in trust, the library left to the town of Quincy more than seventy years ago by John Adams,

BOSTON PUBLIC LIBRARY — Dartmouth and Boylston Streets.

second president of the United States. Another recent gift is that of the Hon. Mellen Chamberlain, librarian of the Public Library from 1878 to 1890, who gives a remarkable collection of autographs and manuscripts. Close upon these last-mentioned additions, another valuable contribution to the library's treasures comes in the shape of a collection of musical works, numbering 7,000 volumes, by Mr. Allen A. Brown.

The New Library Building.—The building in which this magnificent library is housed is one of the few public buildings in America which may be said to be worthy of its purpose. It is deserving of note that neither individual beneficence nor State or national aid have contributed to its erection. It has been built, and it will be adorned, by the city of Boston for her citizens, who, from the Back Bay millionaire down to the humblest among them, will be entitled to enjoy its treasures of art and literature. Although it has been open but a few months, it has undoubtedly taken the leading place as one of the sights of Boston. In the Italian Rennaissance style of architecture, it is quadrangular in shape and surrounds a court. With its platform, it covers, exclusive of the court, an acre and a half of ground. Its walls are of Milford granite, which has a faint pink tinge, and the roof is of brown Spanish tiles. The chief characteristics of the building are its simplicity and the accenting of the horizontal lines of composition. The front consists of a strongly marked first story supporting an arcaded second story, which is surmounted by a massive and projecting cornice, the whole unbroken for 225 feet. The whole structure rests on a low platform, approached by wide encircling steps, which lifts the library above the level of Copley Square. Above the main entrance, and under the three central windows, are carved medallions bearing the seals of the State, the city, and the library. The three arches of the main portal admit us to a vestibule with Tennessee marble walls and inlaid pavement. The three great doorways open into the entrance hall. The main feature of this hall is the lofty arched ceiling of marble mosaics of white and delicate brown tesseræ. The designs are of Rennaissance scrolls surrounding ·tablets, upon which are wrought the names of prominent Americans who have in some way been identified with Boston. The list contains Garrison, Phillips, Sumner, and Mann ; Gray, Bowditch, Agassiz, and Rumford ; Stuart, Copley, Allston, and Bulfinch ; Motley, Prescott, and Bancroft ; Story, Shaw, Webster and Choate ; Eliot and Mather, Channing and Parker ; Longfellow, Hawthorne, Peirce, Adams, Emerson, and Franklin. The floor of this hall is in white and Breccia marbles, inlaid with brass. At the foot of the stairway the design in the inlay is a laurel wreath surrounding the names of the benefactors of the library—Bates, Everett, Quincy, Bigelow, Vattemare, Jewett, and Winthrop.

Opposite the entrance rises a monumental staircase, the steps of Echaillon marble, and the sides of richly colored Siena marble in large sheets. At the wide landing, guarding the stairs on either side, are the couchant marble lions, by St. Gaudens. These were the gifts of the 2d and 20th Massachusetts Volunteer Infantry, in memory of their comrades who fell in the Civil War. At the landing double oak doors open upon a balcony which overlooks the interior court. From the landing the staircase branches into two stately flights that end upon a columned gallery, which at either end is continued into lobbies. That on the right leads to the waiting-room; that on the left to the room for relics. The gallery also opens directly into Bates Hall, the great general reading-room, which stretches across the whole front of the building, and is lighted by its main range of windows. This noble room, 217 feet in length, 42 feet in breadth, and 50 feet to the crown of its barrel-vaulted ceiling, containing half a million books, speaks eloquently of the multitude of readers the library serves.

The central court is inclosed by the four wings of the building, and is entered through the Boylston Street portal. It is encircled on three sides by graceful columnar arcades of marble, above which rise walls of yellowish brick, warm and rich in tone. The calm, pure beauty of its shadowy arcades, the nobility of its solid upper walls, and its air of cloistered seclusion, make it one of the most impressive features of the building. Seats will be provided beneath its arcades and under protecting awnings, and during the warm months of the year it will be an ideal place for study.

" Its projectors knew," says a recent writer, "that architectural beauty can not be completed without the help of the sister arts; that a worthy house for Boston's books could not be built unless painter and sculptor should give the architect their aid. But they also knew that the building's mission was to spread and encourage knowledge ; they felt that an intimate acquaintance with beauty is one of the most precious and fructifying kinds of knowledge ; and, realizing that this, in most of its branches, can not be acquired from books, they determined to reinforce the voice of books with the voice of art itself."

Decorations.—It will be long before the work of decorating Boston's library is complete ; but a great beginning has been made. There are still to come the immense sculptured groups by St. Gaudens, the bronze doors by French, the colossal stairway decorations by Puvis de Chavannes, and the fountain by Macmonnies, not to mention the large areas of wall and ceiling ultimately to be decorated by the leading painters of America.

The decorations by Puvis de Chavannes, representing the *Muses greeting the Genius of Enlightenment*, are finished and will soon be in the panels and line the gallery of the staircase hall. The composition is divided in the upper part into five high arches, to correspond to those on the wall where it will be placed. In the center of the lower part the panel is interrupted by the frame of a door, over which it is to be set in the stairway of the library. The artist has made the most of these architectural features. His foreground consists of the turfy summit of a cliff, beyond which the eye perceives the open sea. Interspersed here and there in the greensward are heather and oak plants, while the crest of the cliff is bordered with a transparent curtain of young trees, the light contours of which stand clearly out upon the cerulean mass of the ocean.

In the center of the composition a naked youth, representing the Genius of Enlightenment, with extended wings, rests upon clouds, his outstretched hands holding rays of light. To the right and left the yellowish white sky, studded with opaline gleams, dominates the deep blue sea. In the distant horizon, projecting their noble forms upon the pale gold sky, the Nine Muses, chastely draped, rise from both sides of the grassy turf, tuning their lyres and offering palms to the Genius. Some of the Muses take their flight from the soil; others float upon the azure with a graceful unrestraint, like divine butterflies, their white draperies loosely adjusted. One of these Muses, at the left, is exquisite. Raising gently the long veil that covered her sleeping head, she awakes, and mounts straight in the heavens, as though impelled by an unknown force.

The door-frame occupies the center of the turf, and at each side is an allegorical figure, two statues representing Contemplation and Study, who mount guard at both sides of the door and form a natural transition between the ideal landscape and the reality. The first figure is meditative and thoughtful ; the other fixes her regard upon a book that she holds open upon her knees.

Edwin A. Abbey's frieze for the delivery-room is only half completed. The subject of these pictorial presentations is " *The Quest of the Holy Grail.*"

1. The first represents the appearance of the Grail to the infant Galahad, who has been left, after the death of his mother, a descendant of Joseph of Arimathea, in a secluded convent to be brought up by the nuns. The holy maid, who holds the babe aloft in her arms, feels the presence of the vision, but she does not see it. The angel bearing the Grail floats upon widespread wings in celestial white.

2. The second picture shows the young Galahad, in his red robe, kneeling in the convent chapel at the close of the all-night vigil which he is required to keep before starting out on his adventures. Perceval and Bors kneel behind Galahad, fastening his spurs. They are dressed in chain-armor, with low-pointed helmets.

3. The third painting represents the Round Table of King Arthur. The vast circular hall, blazing with light, is filled with knights, each in his appointed seat, and all holding up the hilts of their swords, as if to swear to some great vow. The king stands, dressed in royal purple and gold, under a rich baldachin, with grotesque Celtic heads carved upon it, and pillars of mosaicked marble, like those in the churches of Salerno and Ravello. One seat alone is vacant, the chair of destiny, in which whoever sits must lose himself. An aged man enters, leading Galahad, whom he proclaims as the hero who shall achieve the adventures of the Holy Grail.

4. In the fourth painting we see knights, composing the host of the Grail, under the leadership of Galahad, assembled in the cathedral to receive the episcopal benediction before setting out on their wanderings.

5. The fifth and last completed painting in the series represents the castle of Amfortas, the Fisher King of the legend, who has been wounded centuries ago for his failure to keep the law of purity, which is binding on the Guardian of the Holy Grail. Under an enchantment, he and his court are sustained by a

GRAND STAIRCASE, PUBLIC LIBRARY — Lions by St Gaudens.

Martin L. Hall & Co.

Wholesale Grocers

13 AND 14 SOUTH MARKET,
33 AND 34 CHATHAM STS.,

A. J. ADAMS.
FRED P. VIRGIN.
CHAS. G. BURGESS.

 BOSTON.

shadowy life, while the procession of the Grail passes nightly before their eyes. They can not be released by death until the unstained hero comes into the castle, and, by asking the meaning of the Holy Grail, breaks the spell. Galahad has arrived at the Court of the Wounded King, and is surrounded by its unearthly inhabitants. Amfortas lies in the center upon his couch, which is an ancient Celtic coffin, with a bear's skin thrown over it. His eyes are fixed on the procession of the Grail, which passes before him. Galahad stands absorbed in the wonder of the vision, but fails to ask the question by which alone the spell can be dissolved, and the quest of the Grail be achieved.

John S. Sargent's decorations will depict the " *Religions of the World.*" The work now finished is but a fragment in a scheme of decoration which is to occupy all the available space in the large, lofty, and narrow hall, with a barrel-vaulted ceiling at the top of the building.

The present decorations have for their theme the confusion which fell upon the children of Israel when they turned from the worship of Jehovah to that of the false gods of heathen nations. The composition in the lunette represents the children of Israel beneath the yoke of their oppressors, into whose hands the Lord had delivered them. On the left stands the Egyptian, Pharaoh; on the right the Assyrian king, both monarchs with arms uplifted to strike with scourge and sword. The Israelites, naked in their slavery, bow in submission; their central figure lifts his arms in prayer for deliverance, and behind the yoke a multitude of supplicating hands are raised in imploration to the Lord, to whom his repentant people are making burnt-offering upon the altar. He has heard their prayer; flaming seraphim fly before the face of the Lord, and supply a superb decorative motive with the crimson of their wings, which alone symbolize their presence. His face is invisible, but His mighty arms reach down from the cloud and stay the hands of the oppressors. Behind the Assyrian king stands a protecting genius, with the body of a man and the head of a vulture, holding in one hand a bow, and in the other two arrows. Beside this figure is the Assyrian lion, with two ravens attacking a prostrate corpse. The things symbolize the Assyrian cultus. Among the deities attending the Egyptian monarch is one with a lion's head and wings of black and gold. Prostrate victims beneath the feet of both Assyrians and Egyptians represent the other nations that were oppressed by them. The Assyrian ravens are balanced on the Egyptian side by vultures preying upon the dead.

In the ceiling are represented the pagan deities, the strange gods whom the children of Israel went after when they turned from Jehovah. Underlying all the figures that populate the ceiling is the gigantic, dark, and shadowy form of the great goddess, Neith, the mother of the universe, the goddess whose temple at Sais, in Lower Egypt, was once the center of wisdom for Greece. The feet of Neith touch the cornice on one side, her uplifted hands that of the other, and her overarching figure constitutes the firmament, whose stars are seen through the ring of the zodiac, which forms a collar for the goddess.

The third great division of the work is the frieze of the Prophets. This symbolizes the foundation of the religion of Israel upon the structure of the law. Moses is the central figure, and, in his priestly robes and symbols, is treated conventionally to typify the authority upon which the faith is based. Moses, with the tablets of the Commandments, is modeled in strong relief; the other Prophets are painted on a plane surface. On the right of Moses stands Daniel; on the left, Joshua. The other Prophets, in their order from left to right, are Zephaniah, Joel, Obadiah, Hosea, Amos, Nahum, Ezekiel, Jeremiah, Jonah, Isaiah, Habakkuk, Micah, Haggai, Malachi, and Zachariah.

Other Libraries.

The Boston Athenæum Building is on Beacon Street, between Tremont and Park streets, and is a freestone structure in the later Italian style of architecture, which was built over fifty years ago. The Athenæum originated in a literary club, formed among a set of young men, in 1804, called the Anthology Club, which, for a while, edited and published a magazine called the *Monthly Anthology*. In 1806 they established a reading-room, and a year later obtained an act of incorporation under the present title. For some years the club sustained a library, a museum of natural history, and an art gallery. But the founding of other societies devoted to these different objects, led the Athenæum to transfer to them its various collections, retaining only its valuable library and a few pictures, busts, and statues for decoration. Here will be found a delightful reading-room, and, while the right to use it is confined to the shareholders and their families, great liberality is shown to scholars and strangers, who are always welcomed with courtesy. The library contains 177,298 volumes, many of them valuable and rare. One of its most interesting collections is the library of George Washington, purchased, in 1848, at a cost of $5,000. The scientific library of the American Academy of Arts and Sciences — founded in 1780 — is here, and occupies the eastern room on the lower floor. The Washington statue, in the vestibule, is by Houdon, and is a copy of that at Richmond, Va. (See American Academy of Arts and Sciences, Chapter VIII.)

The **Boston Medical Library Association** occupies the house at No. 19 Boylston Place. Here are reading-rooms, a hall for the meetings of the leading medical societies of the city, and the library of nearly 20,000 volumes and 12,000 pamphlets. This library receives regularly over 300 periodicals.

The **Congregational Library** is to be found in the Congregational House, corner of Somerset and Beacon streets. It contains, in the regular series, over 30,000 volumes. It is open to all for reference.

The **General Theological Library**, No. 6 Mount Vernon Street, contains 15,000 volumes, generally of a theological or religious character. There is a fine reading-room in connection with it.

The **Library of the Massachusetts Historical Society** is housed in the society's rooms on Tremont Street, next to the Boston Museum Building. The library contains nearly 37,000 books, 94,000 pamphlets, and 738 bound volumes of manuscripts, besides several thousand single manuscripts. Among the treasures of the library is the Dowse collection of Americana, bequeathed to the society by the late Thomas Dowse of Cambridge. Here, also, is to be found the largest collection in the country of books relating to the Civil War. Among the valuable manuscripts are the letters and papers of Timothy Pickering, Gen. William Heath, the Trumbull and Belknap papers, manuscripts relating to the French in Canada, and two volumes of John Winthrop's Journal.

The **Library of the New England Historic-Genealogical Society** contains about 25,000 volumes and 70,000 pamphlets. It is located in the rooms of the society, at 18 Somerset Street, just below Ashburton Place. The library and archives of the society are freely open to the public, and are much utilized by persons hunting up their genealogies.

The **Natural History Museum Library**, in the building of the Boston Natural History Society, Boylston Street, corner of Berkeley, contains over 20,000 volumes.

The State Library of Massachusetts occupies quarters in the State House. It is composed largely of volumes of statutes of the different States, Territories, and the United States; the acts of the British Parliament, and the French Archives Parlimentaires; and it also contains valuable legal documents, law reports, works on political economy, education, and social science. The number of volumes is over 10,000. The library is open daily for the use of the Governor and other officers of the State, members of the Legislature, and the general public, under certain conditions. All persons may use it for consultation or reference. Its conduct is under the direction of a board of trustees.

The Social Law Library is in the court house, on Court Square. It was incorporated in 1814, and contains 20,000 law books. The library is open, under certain conditions, to members of the bar and other professional men.

The Museum of Fine Arts.

The Museum of Fine Arts was founded in 1870, and was opened in the building of the Boston Athenæum. Its substantial, but somewhat gaudy, building is at the corner of St. James Avenue and Dartmouth Street, and faces Copley Square. The first section of this building was opened in 1876, and three years later the façade on Copley Square was finished. In 1890 the building was increased to nearly double its original size, and extensive improvements made in the older parts, at a cost of over $250,000, contributed by generous citizens. The architecture is the Italian Gothic, and the material brick, with moldings, copings, and trimmings of red and buff terracotta, imported from England. The building forms a quadrangle surrounding an inner court, and, eventually, it will cover twice the present area by successive extensions toward the south. Two large reliefs on the façade represent two allegorical compositions: "The Genus of Art" and "Art and Industry." The main front has a projecting portico in the center, with polished granite columns.

The institution has been entirely supported by the generosity of its friends, and by private subscriptions. The only gift it has received from the city or State is the land which it occupies. The nucleus of the collection was formerly the property of the Athenæum, and consisted of paintings and casts, and a few gifts from citizens. When the museum was opened, the collection of casts was increased by a number purchased with the proceeds of a sale of pictures, bequeathed by Charles Sumner, and by other gifts. At the present time the casts number nearly 1,000.

The museum has grown, in twenty-five years, to be one of the great museums of the world. In the department of Eastern art, and especially Japanese art, it is very strong. In the department of classical antiquities, and in the department of prints, it has no rival in this country. Six galleries are devoted to the collection of pictures in oil and water-colors, containing many productions of the early American and modern French schools. Ten galleries and corridors are devoted to the immense collection of casts from the antique.

Three cabinets are devoted to exhibitions of engravings. There are galleries of textile arts, of pottery and porcelains, of bronzes, jewelry, coins, and metal work; of wood-carvings, of ivory carvings, of furniture, arms and armor, tapestries, glass, etc., and there is a rich collection of Egyptian art.

The museum contains the school of drawing and painting, with a faculty of seven instructors, and an extensive library of art books. The administration is vested in a board of trustees, representing Harvard University, the Boston Athenæum, and the Massachusetts Institute of Technology, comprising, also, ex-officio the mayor, the superintendent of schools, a trustee of the Lowell Institute, the president of the trustees of the Public Library, and the secretary of the State Board of Education.

Recent bequests have provided a fund of $100,000 for the purchase of modern paintings. The first investments under these bequests have been a portrait by Sir Joshua Reynolds, and Eugene Delacroix's "Lion Hunt." At the same time the department of classical antiquities secured the best collection of Greek vases ever brought to the United States. The museum is open free to the public on Saturdays and Sundays; on other days a fee of 25 cents is charged. Sunday is the great day for the crowd; the poorer people then turn out in vast numbers, and throng all the galleries and cabinets. The behavior of the visitors on these occasions has never been otherwise than admirable.

It would be impossible to thoroughly enjoy the collections without the two valuable historical and descriptive catalogues, which may be had at the entrance for 25 cents.

VII.
CHURCHES AND RELIGIOUS AND BENEVOLENT WORK.

Sunday in Boston.— The Puritan Sunday is a matter of history, which it is as hard for the present generation to understand as the religious persecution which darkens the early annals of this fair town. We may turn from the old laws, which forbade any work "except for necessity or charity," to a Sunday edition of one of the great daily newspapers, and read that one of Boston's prominent clergymen will hold a special service of morning prayer for the benefit of those persons who wish to spend the remainder of the day in the enjoyment of out-door life and recreation. It is not that Boston has grown to be a wicked city; quite the reverse. It only proves that her intellectual and spiritual development have, like her material growth, been upon broad and humanitarian lines; and that the mental, moral, and physical needs of individuals are considered together. It is certainly more Christlike to send the weary toiler from the shop or factory for a run on the bicycle through the green fields, for a sail on the blue waters of the bay, or for a stroll with wife and children through the beautiful parks, than to confine him in the house from sundown Saturday night until Monday morning, with no change except to the hard seats of the meeting-house, and the long, doctrinal sermons of the early fathers. And so, while the day is generally observed, and the services of the many churches are well attended, healthful recreation is not only permitted, but provided, by the city government. The means and principal places of worship will be described below; in addition to them, irregular services may be found advertised in the newspapers, where, also, the hours of meeting and the subject of the next day's sermons are announced for many of the leading churches. The Museum of Fine Arts and the

(98)

Public Library are open during the usual hours. Most, if not all, of the excursion boats which, in summer, ply between Boston and the seaside resorts, make their ordinary trips, and these places are more crowded upon this than upon any other day of the week. The parks offer unrivaled facilities for quiet enjoyment, and are easily reached by electric cars from different parts of the city. All places for the sale of liquor are closed by law during the twenty-four hours from midnight of Saturday to midnight of Sunday, and business generally is suspended.

Protestant Churches.

Every denomination of Christians is represented in Boston. There are nearly 300 places of worship in the city, and in all of them strangers are welcome, and are cheerfully provided with seats, so long as there are any vacant. Services in the Protestant churches begin in the morning, generally at 10.30 ; and in the evening at 7.30. The Roman Catholic churches celebrate high mass and vespers at about the same hour. Nothing is implied in the order in which the denominations are mentioned herein, except that it seems suitable to begin with the oldest.

The **Congregational Unitarian** denomination has the honor of possessing the oldest Protestant organization in Boston. *The First Church of Boston* was organized by John Winthrop, Thomas Dudley, and other leaders of the Colonists, in Charlestown, under a great oak, in the summer of 1630. It was given the name of the "First Church of Christ in Boston," when they moved over to the neighboring peninsula. The first meeting-house, with mud walls and thatched roof, stood on the south side of State Street, about where Brazer's Building now stands. The present edifice, on the corner of Berkeley and Marlborough streets, is the fourth building occupied by this society. It is a highly ornamented stone building, with a rich and tasteful interior. It seats about 1,000 persons. John Wilson was the first minister of the church, and John Cotton the second. It became Unitarian toward the close of the long service of Charles Chauncy, who was minister from 1727 to 1787. Rev. William Emerson, father of Ralph Waldo Emerson, was minister from 1799 to 1811. Rev. Rufus Ellis was pastor from 1853 until his death, September 23, 1885. Present pastor, Rev. Stopford Wentworth Brooke.

The second church established in Boston is represented by the

Second Unitarian Church, in Copley Square. The society was organized in 1649, and has occupied six different meeting-houses. In the belfry of the third meeting-house hung the first bell cast in Boston, made by Paul Revere, in 1792. The first minister of the church was Rev. John Mayo. Rev. Increase Mather was the second, his service covering fifty-nine years (1664-1723). During the greater portion of this period, Cotton Mather was his colleague (1685-1728); and Samuel Mather was minister from 1732 to 1741. The first Unitarian minister was Rev. John Lathrop (1768-1816). Succeeding pastors were Revs. Henry Ware, Jr., Ralph Waldo Emerson, Chandler Robbins, Robert Laird Collier, and Edward A. Horton. Present pastor, Rev. Thomas Van Ness, installed in 1893.

Another prominent church of this denomination is the *Church of the Disciples*, on Warren Avenue, which was founded by the late James Freeman Clarke, in 1841, " to embody the three principles of a free church, a social church, and a church in which the members, as well as the pastor, should take part." Rev. Charles G. Ames is the present pastor. The present meeting-house was dedicated in 1869. *The Church of the Unity*, on West Newton Street, near Tremont, of which the Rev. Minot J. Savage is the pastor, dates from 1857, and is one of the most active churches in the city in the prosecution of all good works. The *Arlington Street Church*, on the corner of Arlington and Boylston streets, is a successor of the old Federal Street Church, organized in 1724, under the Presbyterian form. It became Unitarian in 1786. The exterior of the building is plain, with a well-proportioned tower and steeple, placed in the middle of the front. The interior is modeled after the Church of S. Annunziata, at Genoa, by Giacomo Della Porta. A fine range of Corinthian columns divides it into a nave and two aisles. In the tower is hung a chime of sixteen bells, a gift from the late Jonathan Phillips. The list of pastors of the church is short and distinguished : Belknap, John S. Popkin, Wm. Ellery Channing, Ezra S. Gannett (first as associate with Channing from 1824 until the latter's death), John F. W. Ware, Brooke Herford, and John Cuckson, the present pastor.

Congregational Trinitarian.—This denomination stands at the head of Protestant organizations in Boston in the number of its churches. Among its forty-two societies, that of the *Old South* is the most ancient. [For description of the Old South Meeting-House, see Chapter IV.] This was the third church established in Boston, and

ARLINGTON STREET CHURCH — Corner Boylston and Arlington Streets.

SKINNER · & · ARNOLD

No. 28 Faneuil Hall Square

BOSTON, MASS.

•••

WHOLESALE AND RETAIL DEALERS IN CHOICE

. CUTS OF .

Swift's
Chicago
Dressed
Beef...

Pork, Lard, Hams, Bacon,

Tripe, Tongues, Pigs Feet, etc.

HOTEL AND RESTAURANT SUPPLIES .

TELEPHONE CONNECTION

was "gathered" in 1669. Its present home, the *New Old South Church*, is the costly and imposing edifice on Boylston, corner of Dartmouth Street, and is one of the striking features of Copley Square. It is built of Roxbury and Ohio stone, in the Northern Italian Gothic style of architecture. It is cruciform, and has a great tower which rises 240 feet. From this tower an arcade, which shelters memorial tablets, extends to the south transept. Along the walls is a belt of gray sandstone, on which are carved the representations, vines, and fruit, among which animals and birds are seen. Over the center of the edifice rises a large lantern of gilded copper, with twelve windows. The interior is finished in cherry-wood and frescoed. The stained-glass window back of the pulpit represents the announcement of Christ's birth to the shepherds. The south transept window illustrates the five parables; that in the north transept, the five miracles, and those in the nave, the prophets and apostles. Over the doorways are three panels of Venetian mosaic. The present pastor is Rev. George A. Gordon. *Park Street Church*, marking the corner of Tremont and Park streets, was built in 1809. This was the first Congregational Trinitarian church established after the great Unitarian movement which caused such a breaking up of lines in orthodox ranks. In the early days the singing of the Park Street choir, composed of fifty singers, with flute, bassoon, and violoncello accompaniment, was an attractive feature of the Sunday service. Rev. Isaac J. Lansing is the pastor. *Berkeley Temple*, corner of Berkeley Street and Warren Avenue, is another active society of this faith. It maintains many philanthropic enterprises.

Episcopalian.—The first church of this faith established in Boston was King's Chapel, and the second old Christ Church. [For history and description of these churches see Old Landmarks, Chapter IV.] *Trinity Church*, third Protestant Episcopal church in Boston, was founded in 1728. The present beautiful church edifice in Copley Square is the third building occupied by the society. The building is considered the masterpiece of the great architect, Richardson, and it is open to visitors every day, except Sunday, from 9 A. M. to 5 P. M. The architecture is the French Romanesque. Its shape is that of a Latin cross, with a semicircular apse added to the eastern arm and short transepts. The massive central tower is supported by four piers, close to the angles of the building, and stands on the square at the intersection of nave and transepts. The finial on the tower is 211 feet from the ground. The stone of which the walls of the church are constructed is yellowish Dedham and Westerly granite, with freestone trimmings. The vestibules are finished in oak and ash, and the interior of the church in black walnut. The clear-story is carried by an arcade of two arches. Above the aisles a gallery is carried across the arches, which is called the " triforium " gallery, and connects the three main galleries, one across each transept, and the third across the west end of the nave. The chancel is 57 feet deep and 53 feet wide. It contains beautiful stained memorial windows, a brass lectern, and a marble font.* The decorative work of the interior is by John La Farge. In the great tower are painted colossal figures of David and Moses, Peter and Paul, Isaiah and Jeremiah, with scriptural scenes high above. In the nave is a fresco of Christ and the Samaritan woman.

The building is 160 feet long and 120 feet wide at the transepts. It rests upon 4,500 piles. The great tower weighs over 18,000,000 tons. The chapel is connected with the church by an open cloister. The cost of Trinity, land and building, was $750,000. Trinity Church has had many famous rectors, among them Revs. Samuel Parker, second Bishop of Massachusetts; John Sylvester, John Gardiner, one of the founders of the Athenæum; J. W. Doane, afterward Bishop of New Jersey, and founder of Burlington College; John W. Hopkins, afterward first Bishop of Vermont; Manton Eastburn, fourth Bishop of Massachusetts, and Phillips Brooks, sixth Bishop of Massachusetts. Phillips Brooks' service as rector covered a period of twenty-two years (1869-91). Present rector, Rev. E. W. Donald, installed in 1892.

In the busiest part of Tremont Street, surrounded by modern business buildings, rise the gray granite walls of *St. Paul's Church*, the fourth Episcopal society of Boston. It was built in 1820, and, at that time, "seemed to be a triumph of architectural beauty." Features of the interior are the memorial tablets and the high, old-fashioned pews. The present rector of the church is Rev. John S. Lindsay. The *Church of the Advent*, on the corner of Mount Vernon and Brimmer streets, is of the High Church school. The exquisite music which is rendered by the boy choir of this church is a feature of the Sunday services. There are three services daily throughout the year. The church is open at all times for private prayer. Rev. W. P. Frisby is the rector. There are thirty-three churches of the Protestant Episcopal faith in Boston.

KING'S CHAPEL — Corner Tremont and School Streets.

ALEX. M. POWELL,

Manufacturing
Confectioner

150 and 152 Chambers Street,

New York.

U. S. ARAMELS.
· · High Grade Goods · ·
A Specialty.

The **Baptist** Church in Boston goes back to the days of religious persecution, the first society of the Colony having been established in Charlestown in 1665. It was soon driven to Noddle's Island, now East Boston, which then contained but one dwelling. The first meeting-house was built at the North End, in Boston, on the corner of Salem and Stillman streets, in 1679. The *First Baptist Church*, on the corner of Commonwealth Avenue and Clarendon Street, is the descendant of that society. The church building was designed by the late H. H. Richardson for the society of the Brattle Square Church, and it was purchased by the First Baptist Society in 1882. The main feature of the church is the massive square tower, which is 176 feet high. On the frieze, between the belfry arches and the cornice, are colossal figures in high relief, which were carved by Italian sculptors, from designs by Bartholdi, after the stone had been put in position. The groups represent the four Christian eras, Baptism, Communion, Marriage, and Death. The statues at the corners of the tower typify the Angels of the Judgment blowing their trumpets. The building is in the form of a Greek cross, and the interior is lighted by three rose windows. The Rev. Philip S. Moxom is the pastor. The *Union Temple Church*, a Free Baptist church, was organized in 1839, and long established in Tremont Temple, which was burned in 1893, and has been succeeded by the new Tremont Temple. Dr. George Lorrimer, the present incumbent, has been twice pastor of the church.

The **Methodist Episcopal** church has thirty-two organizations within the city. The *Tremont Methodist Church*, on the corner of Tremont and West Concord streets, is the finest church building belonging to this denomination in the city. It is in the plain Gothic style, and is constructed of Roxbury stone.

The churches of this denomination are to be found in every part of the city, and they are in the van in all missionary and charitable work.

Presbyterianism has not kept pace with other religious sects in Boston, and at present has but nine church organizations. The *First Presbyterian Church*, Berkeley Street, corner of Columbus Avenue; the *First Reformed Presbyterian Church*, on Ferdinand, corner of Isabella Street, and the *Scotch Presbyterian Church*, on Warrenton Street, are among the more prominent societies of the denomination in the city.

Of **Universalist** churches Boston has but ten. The first church was on School Street. Its site is now occupied by the School Street Block. Their present house of worship is on Guild Row, corner of Dudley Street. The *Second Universalist Church* is on Columbus Avenue, corner of Clarendon Street. This has been the pulpit of Rev. Dr. Alonzo A. Miner since 1848. His predecessor was Rev. Edwin H. Chapin, the famous preacher and lecturer.

The **Israelitish** population of the city is centered in the old North End, and most of their synagogues, numbering thirteen, are located in that part of the town. The oldest Jewish society, that of the "Ohabei Shalom," has for its synagogue the old South Congregational Church at 11 Union Park Street. The Temple of Adath Israel is on Columbus Avenue, corner of Northampton Street. It is a handsome Romanesque building of brick, brown stone, and terra-cotta, and contains six hundred sittings. It is the principal synagogue in Boston.

Some miscellaneous churches should be mentioned. The *Working Union of Progressive Spiritualists* occupy the "Spiritual Temple," corner of Exeter and Newbury streets. This is the first meeting-house for Spiritualists erected in the city. It was built in 1885, and its cost, $250,000, was met by Marcellus J. Ayer, a wealthy merchant. The oldest *Swedenborgian Church* in the city is a picturesque Gothic house on Bowdoin Street. This society was organized in 1818. The Salvation Army has meeting places at 7 Green Street, and 2058 Washington Street. The *People's Church*, corner of Columbus Avenue and Berkeley Street, is a free church, and the aim of its supporters is to make it attractive to all classes of people. The seating capacity is from three to four thousand. This church was largely the conception of the Rev. J. W. Hamilton, a Methodist clergyman. The *Christian Scientists* occupy the *First Church of Christ*, on Falmouth Street, corner of Norway. The *Latter Day Saints* worship at 1821 Washington Street. The *Friends' Meeting House* is on Townsend, near Warren Street, Roxbury District. The *Seventh Day Adventists* are located at 26 Union Park Street.

Roman Catholic Churches.

Roman Catholicism met with many obstacles in its efforts to gain a foothold in Boston. But, when once established, its growth was steady and rapid, and to-day it probably leads all other sects in the

TRINITY CHURCH — Boylston and Clarendon Streets.

10

GREAT WESTERN
CHAMPAGNE.

A Natural, Genuine Champagne of the Finest
Quality Produced in America.

number of its communicants. It has forty-two churches, outnumber-
ing, in this particular, every Protestant denomination except the
Congregational Trinitarian. In all charitable and benevolent work,
it is fully abreast of the times. Mass was first celebrated in Boston
in November, 1788, in a building which stood on the present site of
the School Street Building. This was the old Huguenot meeting-
house, built in 1704. Afterward it became the meeting-house of a
congregation of independent worshipers, and, finally, the first Catholic church.

The *Cathedral of the Holy Cross*, on the corner of Washington
and Malden streets, is the largest and most noteworthy Catholic
church in New England. It is constructed of the variegated Roxbury stone, and the architecture is the early English Gothic. The
massive towers will eventually be surmounted by spires, respectively
300 and 200 feet high. The cathedral, with its chapels, covers more
than an acre of ground, and it has a seating capacity of 3,500. The
interior of the church is divided by rows of bronzed pillars, which
support a high clear-story and an open timber roof. The large windows are filled with stained glass, representing various scriptural
scenes and characters. The chancel windows show the Crucifixion,
the Nativity, and the Ascension; and those of the transept, each
covering 800 square feet, represent the "Finding of the True Cross,"
and the "Exaltation of the Cross," by the Emperor Heraclius, after
its recovery from the Persians. The nave is 125 feet high. Beneath
it are class-rooms, chapels, and a crypt for the burial of bishops.
The chancel contains a beautiful altar of variegated marble. The
organ, which is built around the rose window on the west side, is one
of the finest instruments in the country. It has 5,292 pipes and 100
stops. At the northeast corner of the building is the beautiful Chapel
of the Blessed Sacrament, containing the altar of the first Boston
cathedral, which stood on Franklin Street. At the southeast corner
is the Chapel of the Blessed Virgin, and in this is the costly marble
statue of the Virgin. In the cathedral yard is a bronze statue of
Columbus, by Alois Buyens. It is a replica of the San Domingo
monument. It represents the explorer in the attitude of giving
thanks, the left hand raised, and the right pointing to the globe at
his side. The figure and pedestal are twenty-five feet high. The mansion-house of the archbishop and the chief offices of the denomination are on Union Park Street, at the rear of the cathedral.

The **Church of the Immaculate Conception** is on Harrison Avenue, corner of East Concord Street. The church was begun in 1857, and completed in 1861. It is a solid structure of granite, without tower or spire. Above the entrance is a statue of the Virgin Mary, while above all stands a statue of the Saviour. The interior is very fine. It is finished mainly in white, except at the altar end, where the ornamentation is exceedingly rich. On the keystone of the chancel arch is a bust representing Christ; on the opposite arch, over the choir gallery, one representing the Virgin, and on the capitals of the columns are busts of the saints of the Society of Jesus. On the panels of the rich marble altar the life of the Virgin is sculptured; and on either side of the structure are 'three Corinthian columns, with entablatures and broken arches, surmounted by statues of the Immaculate Conception of the Virgin, the whole terminated by a silver cross, with an angel on each side. On the right of the broken arch is a figure of St. Ignatius, and on the opposite side one of St. Francis Xavier. The painting of the Crucifixion, behind the altar, is by Garibaldi of Rome. In the center of the elliptic dome, over the chancel, is a dove with outspread wings. The two side chapels within the chancel are dedicated to St. Joseph and St. Aloysius.

Other Religious Organizations.

There are a great number of missionary and religious societies, both unsectarian and denominational, which do a beneficent work in the city. Some of these are national in character; others purely local. Among these may be mentioned the *Boston Deaf Mute Society*, at 458 Boylston Street, which provides a meeting-place and preaching in sign language, free to all deaf mutes ; the *Clark Street Mission*, which aids and protects discharged prisoners ; the *City Missionary Society*, corner of Beacon and Somerset streets, which provides moral and religious instruction for the poor ; the *Episcopal City Mission of Boston*, No. 1 Joy Street, which does missionary work in the hospitals and prisons, among the sailors, and meets the steamers bringing steerage passengers, and sends visitors into the densely populated portions of the city to labor for the spiritual welfare of the poor ; the *St. Vincent de Paul Society*, 17 Worcester Street, which is active in a variety of religious and charitable work ; the *North End Mission*, 20 Parmenter Street, a society for the elevation of the poor at the North End ; the *Union Rescue Mission*, 34

Kneeland Street, engaged in aiding and lifting up poor, fallen humanity; the *United Society of Christian Endeavor*, 646 Washington Street, a religious society, composed of members of evangelical churches, for the training and guiding of young Christians; the *Order of the King's Daughters*, 7 Temple Place, organized to do "anything that helps another human being to be better and happier, and to develop spiritual life and stimulate Christian activity;" and the *Massachusetts Bible Society*, 12 Bosworth Street, sells or distributes, gratuitously, Bibles and Testaments.

Societies for Social Improvement.

The **Boston Young Men's Christian Association** occupies a handsome building on the corner of Boylston and Berkeley Streets. The object of this society is to provide a homelike resort, with good influences, for young men. The building contains attractive parlors, reception-rooms, reading, game, and class rooms, halls for lectures, and a thoroughly equipped gymnasium. Membership in this association is open to men over fifteen of any religious belief.

The **Boston Young Men's Christian Union**, 45 Boylston Street, is open to young men, over sixteen, of any color or sect. It incites its members to religious and mental culture, and to practical philanthropy. The building has reception-rooms, parlors, a study, library, class and reading rooms, a fine gymnasium, and three public halls. In the largest of these halls — the Union — there are 500 seats, and it has a stage and appliances suitable for amateur dramatic performances.

The **Boston Young Men's Hebrew Association**, 68 Springfield Street, is open evenings. It is devoted to the social and moral advancement of young men.

The **Young Woman's Christian Association**, No. 40 Berkeley Street, was established in 1866. Its object is "to care for the temporal, moral, and religious welfare of young women who are dependent upon their own exertion for support, and to help them in such a way that their self-respect shall not be hurt." It maintains a lodging-house, restaurant, a training-school for domestics, a school of domestic science, evening classes for working girls in dress-cutting, dressmaking, millinery, cooking, typewriting, stenography, and a normal school of physical education, an employment bureau, and a business agency for the various employments open to women.

The **Women's Educational and Industrial Union,** 264 Boylston Street, was established in 1880, and has for its object "to increase fellowship among women, and promote practical methods for their educational, industrial, and social advancement." It maintains a reading-room free to all women of any race or creed; library, classes in bookkeeping, gymnastics, embroidery, millinery, drawing, music, language, etc.; lectures and entertainments on Wednesday evenings in winter, free to men and women; religious meetings on Sunday, for women only, and health talks, by women physicians, twice a week. An agency of direction gives information as to boarding-houses, summer resorts, schools, etc. A befriending committee visits the sick. In the lunch-room a simple bill of fare, at moderate prices, is presented, and women can bring their own lunch to eat here without purchasing.

Charities and Hospitals.

Hospitals.—Boston is one of the foremost cities in the country in the number and equipment of her hospitals. A stranger suffering from illness or accident ought to feel no hesitation in availing himself of the comfort and care provided by these institutions.

The Massachusetts General Hospital, on Blossom Street, had its origin in a bequest of $5,000, made in 1790; but it was not incorporated until 1811. It is the most complete and perfectly organized institution of its kind in the country, and the oldest, save one—the Pennsylvania Hospital. The stately main building, of Chelmsford granite, was designed by Bulfinch. It stands in pleasant shaded ground. It admits, under light conditions, patients suffering from diseases or injuries, from any part of the United States or British Provinces; and provision is made for free treatment, or treatment at the cost to the patient of the expense involved. No infectious diseases are admitted, and chronic or incurable cases are generally refused. On proper call the hospital ambulance, with medical officer, is dispatched, at any hour, to points within the city proper, north of Dover and Berkeley streets. Every arrangement is made, in the hospital, for the treatment, comfort, and happiness of the patient. In connection with this hospital is the *Convalescent Home,* at Waverly, and the *McLean Asylum for the Insane,* also established in Waverly. The hospital maintains a training school for nurses, and a dispensary which gives treatment only.

The names of many men eminent in the medical profession have, at all times, been on the list of its visiting physicians and surgeons. In one of the operating-rooms of this hospital a capital operation was first performed under the influence of ether. (See The ETHER MONUMENT, in Chapter III.)

The Boston City Hospital occupies the entire square between Harrison Avenue, East Concord, Albany, and East Springfield streets, and a part of the adjacent square to Massachusetts Avenue. It is maintained by annual appropriations from the municipal government, and it is governed by a board of trustees representing the government. The hospital staff, consisting of visiting, out-patient, house, departments, and medical and surgical assistants, numbers about seventy. The hospital is chiefly intended for free patients, but there are accommodations for a number of pay-patients, at prices varying from $10 to $30 per week. The hospital proper consists of the central administration building, and eighteen other buildings for patients, forming an effective architectural group. The hospital for contagious diseases, just completed, is known as the Chester Park Hospital, and has accommodations for 260 patients. It is intended for such infectious diseases as diphtheria, scarlet fever, measles, etc. This group of buildings has cost about $350,000, and is the best of any hospital in existence devoted to this special purpose. No American city, save Boston, is provided with a place like this, where gently-nurtured people may have all the comforts and attentions to which they are accustomed. The Convalescent Home, connected with the City Hospital, is at Milton Lower Mills, about four miles from the hospital. It is a. fine old family mansion, which has been extended and enlarged, and accommodates thirty-six patients. It is in a beautiful park of fifteen acres.

The Massachusetts Homœopathic Hospital, on East Concord Street, was incorporated in 1855, but was not established and ready for patients until 1871. For five years it occupied a house at 14 Burroughs Place. The present beautiful building was opened for patients in May, 1876. The funds for its erection were raised by a grand fair, which was held by its friends, and netted nearly $80,000. The hospital has recently been enlarged at a cost of $100,000, and is pronounced, by competent judges, one of the most successful and satisfactory hospitals in the State.

The **Carney Hospital,** on Old Harbor Street, South Boston, was incorporated in 1865. The location is, in every respect, desirable. It stands on Dorchester Heights, and commands an extensive view of Massachusetts Bay, and also of the city. The land on which the hospital stands, and a fund of $53,000, were a gift from the late Andrew Carney. It is in charge of the Sisters of Charity, and is a Catholic institution, but patients of all classes are admitted, no distinction being made on account of creed, color, or race. It is a hospital of the first class, with well-equipped operating-rooms, etherizing-rooms, and other departments.

Other Hospitals.—*Adams Nervine Asylum*, for persons of both sexes affected with nervous diseases, West Roxbury District, Center Street. *Boston Lying-In Hospital*, No. 24 McLean Street. *Channing Home*, for women and children, chiefly incurables, No. 30 McLean Street. *Children's Hospital* for medical and surgical treatment of children, Huntington Avenue, Back Bay District. *Consumptives' Home*, for both sexes, Homœopathic treatment, Roxbury District, corner of Warren Street and Blue Hill Avenue. *Free Hospital for Women*, for treatment of diseases of women, No. 60 East Springfield Street. *House of the Good Samaritan*, for the treatment of women and children, especially incurables, No. 6 McLean Street. *New England Hospital for Women and Children*, under the charge of women. It offers young women studying medicine opportunities for clinical study which other hospitals afford to young men; Codman Avenue, between Washington and Amory streets. *Small-pox Hospital*, near rear entrance of Forest Hills Cemetery, Canterbury Street. *Special Home*, for both sexes afflicted with spinal diseases, homœopathic treatment, Roxbury District, corner Warren Street and Blue Hill Avenue. *St. Elizabeth's Hospital*, for women, No. 78 Waltham Street. *St. Joseph's Home for Sick and Destitute Servant Girls*, for incurables especially, Nos. 41 to 45 East Brookline Street. *St. Mary's Lying-In Hospital* (and Infant Asylum), Dorchester District, Bowdoin Street. *United States Naval Hospital*, connected with the Charlestown Navy Yard, Chelsea.

Other Public Institutions which come under the jurisdiction of the city government, are the *Houses of Industry and Reformation*, and the *Truant School* at Deer Island; the *House of Correction* and *Lunatic Hospital* at South Boston, the *Almshouses* at Rainsford and

Long Islands, and Charlestown; the *Marcella Street Home* for neglected boys and girls, and the *Parental School*, at West Roxbury.

The Associated Charities of Boston.—The objects of this society are to secure the concurrent and harmonious action of the different charities in Boston, in order to raise the needy above the need of relief, prevent begging and imposition, and diminish pauperism ; to encourage thrift, self-dependence, and industry through friendly intercourse, advice, and sympathy, and to aid the poor to help themselves ; to prevent children from growing up as paupers, and to aid in the diffusion of knowledge on subjects connected with the relief of the poor. To accomplish these objects, it provides for the thorough investigation of the case of every applicant for relief, and places the result of such investigation at the disposal of the Overseers of the Poor, of charitable societies and agencies, and of private persons of benevolence. It makes all relief conditional upon good conduct, and sends friendly visitors into the families of the poor. Their offices are in the Charity Building, on Chardon Street.

The Private Charities of Boston are numerous and efficient. They meet almost every want to which suffering humanity is subject, and they are conducted with rare intelligence and devotion. It would be impossible, in a work of this character, to mention even the more prominent private philanthropies. Information concerning them may be obtained at the Charity Building, on Chardon Street.

VIII.
CLUBS, SOCIETIES, AND MILITARY ORGANIZATIONS.

The social clubs of the city are not of special interest to strangers, since, without an invitation from a member, no one is admitted to their privileges. Boston has many clubs, social, literary, professional, business, and commercial. Some of these clubs have palatial houses, wherein every appliance of comfort and luxury is to be found, but many of them are confined to rooms in some convenient locality.

The following is an alphabetical list of the leading clubs and societies in Boston, with brief remarks:

Algonquin, 217 Commonwealth Avenue. This is one of the leading social clubs. Its membership includes bankers, brokers, merchants, lawyers, etc. It was organized in 1885, and occupies one of the finest and most perfectly appointed club-houses in the city. The exterior, in Italian Renaissance architecture, is of Indiana limestone. The reading-room, library, and billiard-hall are each over eighty feet long, and the dining-rooms and other apartments are convenient and attractive.

Apollo Club, 153 Tremont Street. [See Chapter V.]

Appalachian Mountain, 9 Park Street. The objects of this association are to explore the mountains of New England and the adjacent regions, both for scientific and artistic purposes, and, in general, to cultivate an interest in geographical studies. Its members make frequent expeditions to these mountains, strike out new paths, establish camps, construct and publish accurate maps, and collect all available information concerning the mountain regions.

The Atlantic Yacht, Commercial Wharf.

Boston Architectural, 5 Tremont Place, composed of architects and draughtsmen, and non-professionals interested in the aims of the society.

Boston Athletic Association, Exeter, corner of Blagden Street. [See Chapter V.]

Boston Camera Club, 50 Bromfield Street, composed of amateur photographers, and devoted to the advancement, among its members; of a knowledge of photography in all its branches.

The Boston Art Club's handsome home is at the corner of Dartmouth and Newbury streets. The club entrance is on the Newbury Street side, while the public entrance to the art gallery is on the Dartmouth Street front. The building is in the Romanesque style of architecture, with hexagonal corner tower with a massive projecting balcony.

This club was organized in 1857, with a membership of twenty persons, nearly all of whom were professional artists. In 1874 the club was reorganized and now numbers 137 professional and 650 non-professional members. The objects of the club, as stated in its constitution, are "to advance the knowledge and love of art through the exhibition of its works of art, the acquisition of books and papers for the purpose of forming an art library, lectures upon subjects pertaining to art, and by other kindred means; and to promote social intercourse among its members."

The interior of the house is convenient, sumptuous, and inviting. The exhibition gallery, on the second floor, is 47 by 47 feet, and 18 feet high, and, by the arrangement of the interior of the house, the gallery can be thrown open for public exhibitions without encroaching upon the rooms devoted exclusively to club purposes. The club has a valuable library of works on art and books of reference. Its regular spring, summer, and winter exhibitions are important features of the art season in Boston.

The Boston Society of Decorative Art is located at 222 Boylston Street. The purpose of this society is "to raise the standard of design in hand-wrought work and in manufacture, and to guide all those who use the needle, the brush, or the modeling-tool for decorative ends, to an appreciation of pure form and noble design, so that the objects produced or decorated by these agencies might be beautiful to the eye and satisfactory to the cultivated taste." The rooms of the society are open from 10 A. M. to 5 P. M. on week-days, and many beautiful specimens of decorative work are on exhibition. Admission free.

The **Boston Turn Verein,** 29 Middlesex Street, was organized in 1849, and it is the leading German society in the city. The club-house contains a thoroughly equipped gymnasium, billiard-rooms, bowling alleys, a hall having a seating capacity of 500, and a stage for private theatricals, concerts, and other entertainments; a reading-room and library, and restaurant, parlors, and reception-rooms.

The **Bostonian Society,** Old State House, is an organization to "promote the study of the history of Boston, and the preservation of its antiquities." It has charge of the upper stories of the Old State House, and maintains the rooms on the second floor, with the collection of antiquities there, for public exhibition.

The **Boston Merchants' Association,** 56 Bedford Street, was incorporated in 1880. Its membership represents various branches of business. It has regular standing committees on transportation, arbitration, debts and debtors, and postal facilities, telegraphy, etc. Its annual banquets are features in the mercantile life of Boston.

Boston Chess Club, 18 Boylston Place.

Boston Fencing Club, 20 Beacon Street.

Boston Press Club, 14 Bosworth Street, composed of newspaper proprietors, publishers, editors, reporters, and managers, and persons regularly engaged in literary pursuits.

Boston Yacht Club, 817 East Sixth Street. It is the senior yacht club of Boston, and dates from 1866. Its club-house is at City Point.

Caledonia Club, 694 Washington Street, composed largely of leading Scotch citizens.

Catholic Union, 17 Worcester Street, composed of leading Catholics.

Cecilia, 153 Tremont Street.

Commercial Travelers', 694 Washington Street.

Elysium Club, 218 Huntington Avenue. This is composed of the leading Hebrew residents of the city. The club-house was erected in 1891, and it is, in every way, convenient and attractive.

Mayflower Club, 7 A Park Street, a social club of women, organized, in 1893, to provide comfortable rooms down town, "furnished with periodicals and conveniences for writing, and where a simple lunch may be obtained." The club-rooms are pleasant and comfortably furnished, and the restaurant is especially inviting.

Massachusetts Yacht Club, Rowe's Wharf.

New England Woman's Club, No. 5 Park Street. This is one of the most prominent clubs of Boston. Its organization, in 1868, was closely followed by that of "Sorosis" of New York, but the latter club does not resemble its predecessor in its aims. Sorosis is purely a social club, while the New England Woman's Club is not only social, but has a wide-reaching work in many directions. The Woman's Club was intended as a center of rest and social convenience for women already active in various philanthropic ways to the extent of their ability, with the hope and belief that the time thus economized from fruitless search of each other, or spent socially in a less satisfactory manner, given to this sympathetic intercourse, might turn to still more fruitful use from the reaction upon each other of minds so well trained in varied service, when brought to bear upon the special needs of women.

Paint and Clay Club, 419 Washington Street. This club was founded in 1880. Its constitution requires that members shall be connected with art, literature, or music. It gives occasional receptions and art exhibitions.

The Puritan Club, 50 Beacon Street, composed of young men of social standing and wealth. It has excellent table d'hôte dinners for members, and pleasant dining-rooms for private parties.

Republican Club, 223 Washington Street.

St. Botolph Club, 2 Newbury Street, largely composed of professional men. It was organized in 1880, and the purpose of its projectors was to establish a club similar to that of the Century in New York. Among its members are several of the most distinguished of the liberal clergymen of the city, representative literary men, physicians, journalists, artists, and members of the bar. A feature of the club-house is its large art gallery.

The Somerset Club, 42 Beacon Street. This is the most fashionable and exclusive of Boston's clubs. It has occupied its present quarters since 1872. The house, which was formerly the mansion of the late David Sears, stands on the site of the home of Copley, the famous painter. It is an imposing granite front, "double-swell" house, with convenient and elegant interior. A notable feature is a ladies' dining-room for guests of the members, which is also open to non-members accompanying ladies on club orders.

The Suffolk Club, whose house, at 4½ Beacon Street, is a modest, comfortable, and homelike structure, is a purely social club. Politics do not enter into its plans, but it happens that many prominent Democrats are among its members.

Union Club, 8 Park Street. This club was established during the Civil War, primarily as a political club in support of the Union cause. The house was formerly the home of Abbot Lawrence. It is spacious, well arranged, and furnished, adorned with paintings and other works of art, and provided with a fine library. It has, for many years now, been a purely social club, having abandoned its political features.

The Tavern Club occupies very pleasant quarters at No. 4 Boylston Place, in an old-time mansion, which is adorned with works of art and curiosities, given by members. It is a lunch and dining club of gentlemen who are interested in literature, art, music, etc.

The Temple Club, located at 35 West Street, is the oldest club in the city, having been established in 1829. It is a purely social club, and the membership is small. The club-house presents a plain exterior, but its interior is admirably arranged and equipped for club purposes.

The University Club, 270 Beacon Street, was organized in 1881, and its membership is composed entirely of college-bred men, and includes representatives of all the leading colleges in the country. It occupies one of the most sumptuously appointed club-houses in the city.

The Unity Art Club, 16 Arlington Street.

Union Boat Club, foot of Chestnut Street, on the Charles River. This is, with one exception, the oldest boat club in the United States, having been organized in 1851. It is an exclusively amateur association, no member being allowed to enter into negotiations to row a race for a stated sum of money, nor can the funds of the club be appropriated for prizes.

There are several **Literary Clubs** in Boston which, having no club-houses, meet at some leading hotel. The *Saturday Club* dines once a month, at Parker's. Many celebrated writers have belonged to this club. The *Wednesday Evening Century Club* and the *Thursday Club* are associations in which the professional element is dominant. They meet at the houses of members.

Among the **Professional Societies** may be mentioned the *Boston*

Medical Association, which holds its meetings at 19 Boylston Place; the *Boylston Medical Society* of Harvard University, the *Boston Society for Medical Improvement,* the *Boston Society for Medical Observation,* the *Boston Homœopathic Society,* the *Boston Druggists' Association,* and the *Bar Association of the City of Boston.*

Scientific and Learned Societies.

Boston has many societies devoted to scientific and learned investigations. The most widely known is the **American Academy of Arts and Sciences,** at 10½ Beacon Street. With one exception, this is the oldest scientific society in the country. The object of its founders was "the promotion and encouragement of a knowledge of the antiquities and the natural history of America; the encouragement of medical studies, mathematical disquisitions, philosophical inquiries and discoveries, astronomical, meteorological, and geographical observations, and improvements in agriculture, the arts, manufactures, and commerce." Volumes of its "Memoirs" and "Proceedings" are from time to time published. Its library contains 22,000 volumes.

The **Massachusetts Historical Society,** at 30 Tremont Street, was founded, in 1791, by Rev. Jeremy Belknap and seven associates. Its object is to investigate matters of history, and preserve records and relics illustrating it. Besides the library of 36,300 volumes, 95,000 pamphlets, and several thousand manuscripts, it has quite a museum of interesting relics.

The **New England Historic Genealogical Society,** at 18 Somerset Street, was founded in 1844, and has for its object the study and publication of historical and genealogical facts about New England and her people. The library embraces the largest collection in the country of genealogies of New England families, and many valuable and rare manuscripts. The society publishes the "New England Historical and Genealogical Register," issued quarterly.

The **Massachusetts Charitable Mechanic Association,** Huntington Avenue, corner of West Newton Street, was instituted, in 1795, at the "Green Dragon Tavern." Its primary objects were to relieve the families of unfortunate mechanics, and to assist young mechanics with loans of money, and to promote inventions and improvements in the mechanic arts. It has, for a long period now, held "Triennial Festivals," or public exhibitions. The present exhibition building is one of the largest in the country. Of its three halls,

Mechanics' Hall, seating about 6,000, is the largest. Paul Revere was the first president of this association.

Secret Orders.

All, probably, of the secret orders and societies in the United States have representatives in Boston. Several of these stand before the public more in a social aspect, or otherwise, than on account of any secrecy in their proceeedings, *e. g.*, the Greek letter college societies.

Free Masonry.—The first Masonic lodge in the country was organized in Boston, in July, 1733. The headquarters of the Masonic societies of the city are in *Masonic Temple*, on the corner of Tremont and Boylston streets.

This is an imposing granite building, with octagonal towers rising to the height of 120 feet, while the height of the building proper is 90 feet. The Tremont Street front is 85 feet wide. The structure is seven stories high, and has three large halls for meetings—one finished in the Corinthian style, another in the Egyptian, and the third in the Gothic. The entire building, with the exception of the street and basement floors, is occupied by the Masonic organizations of the city. The corner stone was laid on St. John's day, June 22, 1867.

Odd Fellows.—The first lodge of Odd Fellows in Boston was organized March 26, 1820. It was the second in the country, the first having been established in Baltimore April 26, 1819. The headquarters of the several organizations in the city are in Odd Fellows' Building, No. 515 Tremont Street, corner of Berkeley.

The Benevolent and Protective Order of Elks, No. 24 Hayward Place, is a secret benevolent organization, incorporated in 1879. Its membership, at first composed chiefly of actors, now includes persons from all professions. It gives assistance to members who are ill or out of employment, according to the discretion of a relief committee charged with this duty. It is a national organization, and has lodges in different cities.

Military Organizations.

State Militia.—The headquarters of the *First Brigade* are at No. 19 Milk Street, and of the *Second Brigade* at No. 37 Tremont Street.

The First Corps of Cadets, M. V. M., quite an aristocratic four-company battalion of young men, organized in 1741, and once commanded by John Hancock, are quartered in the castellated granite armory on Columbus Avenue, southeast corner of Ferdinand Street. The *First Regiment of Infantry*, the *Fifth Regiment of Infantry*, and the *First Battalion of Cavalry*, make their head-quarters in the Irvington Street Armory. The *Sixth Regiment of Infantry's* Armory is on Green Street, corner of Chardon; and the *Ninth Regiment of Infantry* is on East Newton.

The Ancient and Honorable Artillery Company is the oldest military organization in the country. It was chartered in March, 1638, as "The Military Company of Boston," and Robert Keayne, one of the chief promoters of the new organization, was its first captain. It was not until 1657 that it became an artillery company, when it was recognized as such by the general court. The title "Ancient and Honorable" was assumed in 1700, first appearing in its records in September of that year. It was styled "ancient" because of its great age, and "honorable" from the fact that some of its earlier members had belonged to the Honorable Artillery Company of London. The company was dispersed by the Revolution, and revived in 1789, when its name and privileges were confirmed by the Legislature. The anniversary of its organization, the first Monday in June, is still celebrated by an annual parade. A sermon is preached to the company, a good dinner is served in Faneuil Hall, and speeches listened to; and thereafter all march to the Common, where the Governor of the Commonwealth delivers to the newly-elected officers their commissions and the insignia of their offices. The company has its headquarters in Faneuil Hall.

IX.

A TOUR OF THE CITY.

In the following pages is presented a single day's itinerary, covering the more important points of attraction in the city proper, and some of those which, from historical or other associations, are always considered in connection with Boston. Of course, it would not be possible, within such limits of time, to linger long at any one point, and many places which would prove interesting must be omitted from such a tour; but if one has but a short time in which to compass the sights and beauties of this historic town, it is believed that a strict adherence to the route here proposed will enable him to cover more ground, and to see more intelligently the places visited.

Washington Street.

Washington Street, starting at Haymarket Square, and traversing the city longitudinally from the old "North End," through Roxbury to Dedham, is the principal business thoroughfare. The corner of Washington and Bedford streets is about in the center of the hotel and theater district, and will be a good point from which to start on our pilgrimage. Here, on the southeast corner, is the great dry goods establishment of R. H. White & Co., occupying a stone structure, and reaching through to Harrison Avenue, in the rear. Keeping on the right side of Washington Street and walking to the north, we pass some of the largest and finest retail stores in the city. The block, from Avon to Summer Street, with the exception of Shuman's corner, is occupied by the handsome freestone store of Jordan, Marsh & Co. On the opposite side of Washington Street, between Temple Place and Winter Street, is the great music publishing house of Oliver Ditson & Co.

Here, on the southeast corner of Milk and Washington streets, is the building of the *Boston Transcript*, the oldest evening newspaper in Boston. On the opposite corner of Milk Street is the *Old South Meeting-House*, which is described in the chapter entitled "Old Landmarks." Here we must pause to enjoy the quaint old sanctuary, and spend a few minutes in viewing the collection of antiquities which are exhibited in the church. The entrance fee is 25 cents, and goes toward the maintenance of the building. On the opposite side of Washington Street is the building of the *Boston Traveller*, the first 2-cent evening newspaper in Boston, and the first to display news bulletins.

Milk Street.

Let us now turn down Milk Street, noting the building on the opposite side, No. 17, which bears a tablet announcing that it marks the site of Benjamin Franklin's birthplace. Among the buildings, many of which are occupied by banks, railroad, and other corporations, the most notable are those of the International Trust Company, its light stone façade ornamented with carving and sculpture, and then the great insurance buildings. At the corner of Devonshire and Milk is the massive granite building of the Equitable Life Assurance Society, full of banks and offices, with the Security Safe Deposit vaults in the basement. Elevators run to the roof, whence there is a magnificent view of the city and harbor. Next our attention is claimed by the white granite building, in the Renaissance style, of the New England Mutual Life Insurance, at the corner of Milk and Congress streets. This building is crowned by colossal statues. Adjoining this the white marble building, with a stone clock-tower, rising 130 feet, and terminating in a graceful spire, is that of the Mutual Life Insurance Company of New York.

Crossing Post Office Square, we must stop long enough to view the ponderous *Government Building*, which faces the square, and fills the space bounded by Milk, Devonshire, and Water streets. The Post Office Department occupies the basement, the ground floor, and part of the second story of the building. In the second story are also the offices of the Pension Agent, the Naval Pay and Internal Revenue Departments, and the Sub-Treasury. The latter is a fine hall, 50 feet high, adorned with rich marbles and costly trimmings.

The United States Courts, the Lighthouse Board, Lighthouse In-
spectors, and the Signal Service Department are all housed in this
building. The exterior walls of the building are of Cape Ann
granite. The façades rise more than 100 feet above the side-
walks, and the whole is a composition of pilasters, columns, and
round-arched windows, proportioned to set off the massive structure.
On the Post Office Square front are the heroic, sculptured groups, in
Vermont marble, by Daniel C. French of Concord. Facing the
building, the left-hand group represents "Labor Protecting the
Family and the Arts "; Labor, a stalwart figure, with his right arm
supported by the horn of the anvil against which he is leaning. Under
his right arm are the mother and child; at his left is a graceful woman
supporting a vase, while at her feet lie sculptured masks and capitals. The group at the right represents "Science Controlling the
Forces of Steam and Electricity." The central figure, Science, rests
her foot on a closed volume — her undiscovered secrets — and sup-
ports on her left arm a horeshoe magnet, with a thunderbolt as an
armature. At her feet crouches a slave, with hands chained to a loco-
motive wheel; about him clouds of steam and fragments of ma-
chinery. At her right is disclosed the Spirit of Electricity, from
whom she throws back her drapery, which has veiled the figure, and
he stands ready to dart forth to "put a girdle round the earth,"
which lies at his feet. These groups are among the best examples of
symbolic sculpture in the country.

Custom House and Vicinity.

After leaving the Post Office, let us turn east on Water and pass
through Liberty Square, with the Mason Building in the middle of
the square, to Broad Street. Turning to the left, and then at Central
Street to the right, we come to the *Custom House*, a solid, dignified
building, in the form of a Greek cross, and the exterior in pure
Doric style. It was begun in 1835, and was twelve years in building.
The walls, columns, and even the entire roof, are of granite, and it
rests upon 3,000 piles. Each of the massive, fluted columns is 5 feet
2 inches in diameter, 32 feet high, and weighs over 40 tons. There
are thirty-two of these columns. The porticoes have each six columns.
The granite dome, at the intersection of the cross, terminates in a skylight, which is 25 feet in diameter. The cross-shaped rotunda, finished
in the Grecian-Corinthian style, is the main feature of the interior.

BOSTON CHAMBER OF COMMERCE — India Street, near Atlantic Avenue.

Just beyond the Custom House, on India Street, is the *Chamber of Commerce Building*, with circular front and lofty, conical roof pierced by high dormer windows. It is Romanesque and irregular in plan, conforming to the shape of the lot. The chamber occupies the entire third floor. The board-room, or exchange, is circular in form, with high domed ceiling — the apex 38 feet above the floor — and has a floor space of 4,300 square feet. The visitors' gallery is over the entrance.

Leaving the Chamber of Commerce and retracing our steps for a short distance, pass to the rear of the Custom House and along Commercial Street to the *Quincy Market*, a long, low, granite building, with porticoes of massive granite columns, and at either end a well-proportioned dome. This market-house (officially called "Faneuil Hall Market") is a monument of the first Mayor Quincy's administration, which covered six terms, 1823-'29. It was built in 1825-6, and cost, exclusive of the land, only $150,000. The building is 534 feet long, extending from Commercial Street to Faneuil Hall Square. A walk through the market, from the east to the west portal, will be found instructive and interesting; while outside, on both the north and south sides of the building, the countless vegetable and market wagons make an animated scene.

Leaving the market by the west portal, you are directly opposite old *Faneuil Hall*, in which every patriotic American feels an interest. [For history and description of Faneuil Hall, see chapter entitled Old Landmarks.] After visiting the "Cradle of Liberty," and viewing the collection of portraits and relics of Colonial and Provincial times, let us pass through Dock Square to Adams Square, where Miss Anne Whitney's *Statue of Samuel Adams* calmly surveys the hurry, and bustle, and crowd of Washington Street. This statue, which is a counterpart of that by the same artist in the Capitol at Washington, was set up in 1880, the 250th anniversary of the settlement of the town. The patriot leader is represented as he is supposed to have looked when he was awaiting Governor Hutchinson's reply to his demand for the instant removal of the British troops from the town, the day after the "Massacre of 1770." Let us now turn up Washington Street, and, keeping on the left side of the street, we must take time to admire the lofty *Ames Building*, on the northwest corner of

Court and Washington streets. This is the tallest building in the city, and, covering a very small area, its granite walls rise to a height of 190 feet. This finely designed structure cost about $700,000. It was completed in 1890, and its tenants are chiefly banking institutions and lawyers. On the opposite corner of Court and Washington streets is another handsome business block, the *Sears Building*. This is in the Italian Gothic style of architecture, its exterior walls of gray and white marble. Here several great Western railroads and New England manufacturing companies have their offices. Just in the rear of this building, on Court Street, is Young's Hotel; and here, on our left, standing at the head of State Street (in ante-Revolutionary days King Street), is the *Old State House.* [For history and description of the Old State House, see chapter entitled " Old Landmarks."] After completing our inspection of this most interesting relic, let us walk a short distance down State Street, the financial center of the town.

State Street.

Emerging from the Old State House, by the eastern portal, we are confronted on either hand by massive modern buildings. On the north side, at No. 28, is the building of the Merchants' National Bank, the largest banking institution in New England. Just beyond this is the Massachusetts Hospital Insurance Building. On the south side of State Street is the old-fashioned Brazer's Building, which will, doubtless, soon give way to a much larger structure. The ten-story building of light brick, occupying the little block formed by Congress Square and Congress Street, is the Worthington Building, built by Roland Worthington, the former owner of the *Boston Traveller.*

The most notable of the modern buildings of State Street is the mammoth twelve-story granite Stock Exchange, one of the largest office buildings in the country. It has a frontage of 170 feet on State Street and 160 feet on Kilby Street. The cost of this great structure was $4,000,000. In this building are the quarters of the Stock Exchange, at the end of the entrance hall on the first floor. The chamber is a fine hall 115 feet long, 50 feet wide, and 35 feet high, with Corinthian pillars around the sides. Entrance to the visitors' gallery is from the marble hall of the second floor of the building. Looking down from this gallery, the " pulpit," where the chairman sits during the sessions, is seen in the middle of the right side of the room ; beyond it the Boston Stock Board ; and opposite that, on the left side of the room, the New York Board, with a nest of telephone boxes below. Near the "pulpit" is the telegraph room ; and immediately opposite, on the left side, is the entrance to the bond room. In the block beyond the Exchange Building is the solid stone Fiske Building. The brownstone and yellow brick Farlow Building on the corner of Merchant's Row, and the white marble Richards Building, just below, complete the list of great modern buildings on this quaint old thoroughfare.

Newspaper Row.

Retracing our way through State to Washington, and again turning to the left, we are in the midst of the newspaper offices. *Newspaper Row* is the name given to that part of Washington Street between State and School streets. The first of these offices to our left, on the east side of the street, is the handsome freestone structure occupied by the *Globe*. In politics it is Democratic. Just above and adjoining the *Globe* is *The Daily Advertiser's* marble building. It covers the site of the shop and dwelling of James Campbell, bookseller and postmaster, who issued the Boston *News-Letter*, the first newspaper successfully established in North America (1704).

This is the oldest morning paper in Boston, the first number having appeared on March 3, 1813. In politics the *Advertiser* is Republican. In 1884, the *Advertiser* corporation began the publication of *The Evening Record*, a penny evening paper, agreeing with the *Advertiser* in politics. On the same side of the street, near the corner of Water Street, is the building of the *Boston Journal*, a Republican morning and evening paper, which was first published, in 1833, under the name of the *Evening Mercantile Journal*. Its present name was adopted when the publication of the morning edition was begun, in 1837. On the opposite side of Washington Street are the *Herald* and *Post* buildings. The *Boston Herald*, a morning, evening, and Sunday paper, independent in its political relations, was founded in 1846. Its present building, in the French Renaissance style, has been occupied since 1878, and is one of the best equipped offices in the city. Next to the *Herald* Building is the home of the *Boston Post*, a Democratic morning paper, founded by Charles G. Greene, in 1831.

School Street and the City Hall.

A few steps down Washington Street brings us to the corner of School Street, where stands the Old Corner Book Store. [See "Old Landmarks"]. School Street is a short, but crowded, thoroughfare, running from Washington to Tremont Street. On our right is the brownstone and brick front of the *Niles Block*, on the site of the dwelling of Dr. John Warren, first professor of surgery in Harvard University, and brother to Dr. Joseph Warren, one of the heroes killed at Bunker Hill. On the opposite side of the street, where the School Street Block now stands, was the Huguenot Meeting-House, built in 1704, and this same meeting-house, in 1788, was transformed into the first Catholic church. A few steps brings us to the *City Hall*, a white granite building, erected in 1865. It is in the Italian Renaissance style, crowned by a Louvre dome. Within this building are the rooms of the mayor, the halls of the board of aldermen and common council, and other city offices. In the dome is the central point of the fire-alarm telegraph system. In the yard, at the left of the entrance, is a fine bronze portrait statue of *Benjamin Franklin*, by Richard S. Greenough. The statue is eight feet high, and stands on a pedestal of Quincy granite, capped by a block of verd-antique. On the bronze medallions are represented important events in Franklin's life:

South Face.—The boy in the printing office; with this inscription below: "Born in Boston, 17 January, 1706; died in Philadelphia, 17 April, 1790."

North Face.—His experiment with the lightning; with this inscription: "*Eripuit æclo fulmen, sceptrumque tyrannis.*"

East Face.—Signing the Declaration of Independence, 4 July, 1776.

West Face.—Treaty of Peace and Independence, 3 September, 1782.

The statue of Josiah Quincy, on the right, is by Thomas Ball. The figure is heroic, and stands on a pedestal of Italian marble. The pedestal, which was also designed by Ball, bears the following inscription:

JOSIAH QUINCY.

1772-1864.

MASSACHUSETTS SENATE, 1804.

CONGRESS, 1805-1813.

JUDGE OF MUNICIPAL COURT, 1822.

MAYOR OF BOSTON, 1823-1828.

PRESIDENT OF HARVARD UNIVERSITY, 1829-1845.

This statue was erected with money drawn from a trust fund

TREMONT STREET, LOOKING SOUTH FROM PARK STREET.

Entrance to Common.

GOOD COFFEE

established, in 1860, by Jonathan Phillips, who bequeathed to the city $20,000, "the income from which shall be annually expended to adorn and embellish the streets and public places."

King's Chapel [see chapter entitled "Old Landmarks"] is next to the City Hall, while across the street the Parker House [see remarks on "Hotels" in Chapter I] lifts its marble front and fills in the block from Chapman Place to Tremont Street.

Scollay Square and Vicinity.

As we turn into the narrow, crowded thoroughfare of Tremont Street, we notice, on the northeast corner of Beacon and Tremont streets, the great department store of Houghton & Dutton. On our right, after passing King's Chapel and the burying ground, we come to the Boston Museum Building [see Chapter V] and, on the corner of Tremont and Court streets, the brownstone *Hemenway Building*, marking the site of an old house in which General Washington stayed during his visit to Boston in 1789. Scollay Square, an irregular triangle, caused by the removal of the old Scollay Building, is the terminal point of many street car lines from different parts of the city, and from suburban and outlying sections. The main feature of the place is the bronze statue of *Governor John Winthrop*, by Richard S. Greenough. The statue was erected in 1880, and was also paid for out of the Jonathan Phillips fund. It is a duplicate of that standing in the Capitol at Washington. Winthrop is represented as just landed in the New World. In his right hand is the Colony Charter, and in his left the Bible. At his back is shown a newly cut forest tree, with a rope attached, significant of the fastening of the boat in which he is supposed to have come to the shore.

Crossing Scollay Square to the entrance of Pemberton Square, we can see the front of the *County Court House*, which stretches across the entire length of the square. It is a massive granite building, in the German Renaissance style, 450 long, 190 feet in its greatest width, and 85 feet high. The building incloses four court-yards, which have an area of 14,632 feet. About these court-yards are grouped the rooms and corridors. The building covers 65,356 feet. The entrance for judges and jury are in the rear of the building. The imposing entrance hall is ornamented by a series of emblematic statues by Dominga Mora. They represent Law, Justice, Wisdom, Innocence and Guilt. George A. Clough was the architect of this building, which was begun in 1871, and cost $2,500,000.

Keeping to the left around Pemberton Square, we enter Somerset Street, and, turning to the left again, we pass *Jacob Sleeper Hall*, chief building of Boston University. [See " Boston University," in Chapter VI.] At the corner of Somerset and Beacon streets is the *Congregational House*, the headquarters of Congregationalism. Here are the offices of the denominational paper, the museum of the American Board of Commissioners for Foreign Missions, the rooms of the Congregational Club, Pilgrim Hall, and the Congregational Library. Let us walk along Beacon Street to the south. On the east side of the street is the building of the Boston Athenæum, and nearly opposite this the Hotel Bellevue, constructed from several old-fashioned dwellings, and, next beyond this, the massive brownstone *Unitarian House.* Here are the denominational book salesrooms ; offices and committee rooms of the American Unitarian Association, the Unitarian Sunday School Society, which comprehends the whole country, and the Benevolent Fraternity of Churches ; and on the upper floor, " Channing Hall."

At the corner of Beacon and Park streets is the *Raymond Building*, formerly one of the finest houses in the city. It was built, in 1804, by Thomas Amory, and was called "Amory's Folly," because of its great size and costliness. It was at a later period divided into four dwellings. Among the distinguished people who have, at different times, been its tenants, were Gov. Christopher Gore, Samuel Dexter, the great lawyer and statesman, and Edward G. Malbone, the miniature painter. Lafayette stayed here for two weeks, in 1824, as the guest of the city, the house having been rented for this purpose by Mayor Quincy.

Beacon Hill.

The next object to claim our attention is the *State House*, on the highest point of Beacon Hill. This fine old building is approached by a broad flight of stone steps. In the yard, on the right, is a bronze statue of Webster, by Hiram Powers; on the left, one of Horace Mann, by Emma Stebbins. The State House, with its gilded dome, is visible from many parts of the city and harbor. The land on which it stands was Governor Hancock's cow pasture, and was purchased from his heirs by the town and given to the State. The building was designed by Bulfinch, the first and one of the greatest of American architects. The corner-stone was laid by the Free Masons (Paul Revere, Grand Master), July 4, 1795. It was first occupied by the Legislature in January, 1798. In 1853-56, it was extended northerly to Mount Vernon Street, and, a few years later, its interior was remodeled. In 1874. it was extensively repaired, and its dome was gilded, and in 1889, the State's business having outgrown it, the Legislature authorized the construction of the " *State House Extension* " in the rear of the original building.

The extension is of yellow brick, with trimmings of white marble, simulating the familiar yellow and white of the " Colonial " style. Its design was intended to harmonize with that by Bulfinch, but the result is generally regarded as infelicitous, being severely criticised as out of scale and weak in effect, though having the merit of considerable good detail.

The connection has not yet been made with the old part. The commissioners in charge of the construction of the new part last year urged the demolition of the Bulfinch edifice and the con-struction of an entirely new front. This raised such a universal and indignant protest throughout the Commonwealth that the prop-osition was rejected by the Legislature. There is a strong feel-ing that the reconstruction of the old part, made necessary by new conditions, should proceed with the most thoughtful regard for the spirit of Bulfinch's historic design, while making such changes as are essential to protect it against the injurious effect of the ill-con-sidered addition.

The interior of the extension is pleasant, cheerful, well ven-tilated, and, for the most part, convenient. It is occupied by the various administrative and executive departments of the common-wealth, and includes two large and handsome halls — that of the House of Representatives and the State Library, besides various legislative committee-rooms, etc. The Senate remains in its chamber in the old building.

The new Hall of Representatives is a handsome and richly decorated room, considerably larger than the old hall, but lacking the stately beauty of the latter, which is one of Bulfinch's finest interiors. The acoustic properties of the old hall are perfect, but those of the former turn out to be very defective.

The decorations of the new hall, by Mr. Frank Hill Smith, are very handsome. Its amphitheater shape, with domed ceiling, lends itself well to fine decorative effects. The treatment is in the Italian Renaissance. Prominent features of the scheme are the names of fifty-three men, eminent in Massachusetts history, inscribed on the frieze, beginning with John Carver and ending with Phillips Brooks; the names of the counties in the stained-glass skylight, and the symbols of Statecraft, Law, Commerce, Science, Industry, the Arts, etc., that occupy panels in the coving and elsewhere. Five large panels on the wall are intended to be occupied by decorative pictures, representing events in Massachusetts history.

The State House, in its new shape, will have grounds of considerable extent on the east side, a large area, now covered with buildings, having been taken for the purpose.

Visitors will be interested in the collection of statues, battle-flags, and tablets which are displayed in Doric Hall. Among the statues is one of Washington, by Chantrey, and one of Governor Andrew, by Thomas Ball.

Just beyond the State House, in the fence in front of a modern brownstone house, is a tablet announcing that here once stood the *Hancock Mansion*, which, in its day, was one of the finest mansions in the town. Built, in 1737, by Thomas Hancock, it was inherited by his nephew, John Hancock. It was taken down, in 1863, to make room for modern improvements.

At the corner of Beacon and Joy streets is the lofty *Hotel Tudor*, one of the largest and finest apartment houses in Boston. In its rear, No. 1 Joy Street, is the Diocesan House, used by the various organizations of the Protestant Episcopal Church. The house belongs to the Episcopal Church Association.

Through the Common and Public Garden.

Now, let us cross Beacon Street and enter *the Common* by way of the Joy Street gate. By taking the path to the right and skirting the Frog Pond to its western extremity, we shall strike a path leading to the Soldiers' and Sailors' Monument. [See *The Common*, in Chapter III.] Leaving the Common by the Charles Street gate, and crossing the street, we are at once in the midst of the beauties of the *Public Garden*. [See *The Public Garden*, in Chapter III.] If we

COMMONWEALTH AVENUE.

12

follow the main walk across the bridge to the Arlington Street gate, we shall have time to view the beautiful equestrian statue of Washington, and the fountain and Ether Monument to our right.

Commonwealth Avenue.

We now cross Arlington Street and enter the stately boulevard, *Commonwealth Avenue*, with a shady parkway through its center, and palatial homes lining it on either side. We will follow the shady central path and, quite near Arlington Street, we pass the granite statue of Alexander Hamilton, the work of Dr. William Rimmer. This was the gift to the city of Thomas Lee, the donor of the " Ether Monument " in the Public Garden. Just beyond Berkeley Street is the bronze statue of Gen. John Glover, commander of the Marblehead Marine Regiment in the Continental Army. This is Martin Milmore's work, and was presented to the city by Benjamin T. Reed. Crossing Clarendon Street, at the left is the beautiful First Baptist Church, described in Chapter VII. On the southeast corner of Dartmouth Street is the Vendome, its white marble front extending along the avenue a distance of 240 feet. In front of the Vendome in the parkway is a bronze statue of William Lloyd Garrison, the great anti-slavery agitator. The statue is the work of Olin L. Warner of New York. This is one of the best portrait statues in the city. On one side of the pedestal is cut Garrison's daring declaration :

" I am in earnest; I will not equivocate; I will not excuse; I will not retreat a single inch; and I will be heard."

And on the other side:

" My country is the world; my countrymen are all mankind."

Copley Square.

We will now turn back to the corner of Dartmouth Street, and keep on the right side of that street to Copley Square. On the corner of Newbury we pass the Boston Art Club's home, and opposite, on our left, the Victoria Hotel, a brick building with crenelated trimmings and battlemented top.

Here we catch a glimpse of *Copley Square*, the center of artistic, literary, and educational life in Boston. At our right, on the corner of Boylston and Dartmouth, is the new Old South Church. Facing the square is the chaste and classic front of the new Public Library, with

its enormous pedestals at either side of the entrance, waiting for
St. Gaudens' groups, and much of the expanse of its pale walls
covered richly with the names of the world's greatest men.

On the south side is the Museum of Fine Arts, with matchless
treasures of Oriental art, and at the east stands Trinity, with its
beautiful central tower and its quiet cloisters. On the north side of
the square are the Second Unitarian Church, Chauncy Hall School,
and two apartment houses. A recent writer, in speaking of this
most attractive part of the town, says·

" Copley Square, at certain hours of the day, presents the aspects
of a new Latin quarter, so conspicuously does the student element
predominate in the throngs that cover its pavements. Here the
currents intermingle and cross, now tending toward the Massachusetts Institute of Technology, on Boylston Street ('Tech' is the
only name ever given this great scientific school in Boston); now
hurrying toward the Harvard Medical School; now making for the
three busy art schools in the neighborhood — those of the Museum
of Fine Arts, the Massachusetts Normal Art School, the Cowles Art
School; and, eddying aside from the main currents, go the thousands of school-boys and school-girls, bound for the countless public
and private schools of the Back Bay and the South End — one building alone, that of the public Latin and English High Schools, containing nearly 2,000 boys, who come to it from all parts of Greater
Boston."

To Cambridge via Harvard Bridge.

And now we will take an electric car going south on Boylston
Street, with " Harvard Square " on end sign, and visit Harvard College, in Cambridge, but which, in reality, spreads all over Boston. Our
route is along Boylston Street to Massachusetts Avenue and westward across Harvard Bridge. As we cross Commonwealth Avenue
we catch a fleeting glimpse of Miss Whitney's statute of Leif Ericsson
and the Fens. From the bridge we can look back on our right and
see the houses of the Back Bay region. While speeding along Massachusetts Avenue, we must notice on our right, at the corner of Inman
Street, the City Hall, a gift to the city from a former resident. [See
Cambridge, in Chapter II, and *Harvard University*, in Chapter VI.]

In returning to Boston, we take the Scollay Square car, which,
starting from Harvard Square, passes along Kirkland, Cambridge,

and Bridge streets; Craigie Bridge, which affords a good view of Charlesbank [see *Charlesbank*, in Chapter III], Leverett, Causeway, Portland, and Sudbury streets to Scollay Square. Here we will leave this car and board another, which passes along the famous old Cornhill to Adams Square, where Washington Street is entered.

Charlestown and Bunker Hill.

The car crosses Hanover Street to Haymarket Square; passes through Beverly Street, and then across the broad bridge to Charlestown. On the right, as we cross the bridge, we have glimpses of the harbor and shipping, while on our left are the railroad bridges. Crossing City Square, with the Waverly Hotel on one side, and the old City Hall of Charlestown ahead, the car runs off on Park Street. As it enters Warren Street, the Navy Yard can be seen down a long street to the right, and just ahead is the Charlestown Soldiers' Monument, the work of Martin Milmore. Three squares beyond, on looking up Monument Street to the right, and at its head, we see the granite obelisk of Bunker Hill Monument. [See *Charlestown* and *Bunker Hill Monument*, in Chapter II.]

Returning by the same route, we shall find ourselves back at the point from whence we started, having covered much of the territory and noted many of the points which, from historical or other fame, are most attractive to visitors.

X.

BOSTON HARBOR AND SEASIDE RESORTS.

The Harbor. — The advantages of Boston Harbor have often been recounted by scientists, and are constantly experienced by those who go down to the sea in ships. The facility and safety of its approaches, the ample width and depth of its entrance, and the shelter and tranquility of its roadsteads, are not surpassed by those of any harbor in the world. Her interior water-space is divided by chains of islands into basins, which offer sufficient room for 500 ships of the largest class to ride freely at anchor, and sufficient tranquility for the frailest pleasure craft. But it is not of these things that the average tourist will think as he stands on the deck of one of the harbor steamboats that ply between the city, and the towns, and the resorts that line the shores on either hand. The surpassing loveliness of the harbor, its surface dotted with numberless islands of fantastic shape, and its irregular and picturesque shores, will hold him spell-bound, and forgetful of scientific data and historical legend.

And Boston has nothing better, in the way of entertainment, to offer to her guests than a sail on the blue waters of her bay. Most of the islands have a history which it would be interesting to review, and those who are tracing resemblances will find amusing the following description by Doctor Shurtleff: " Noddle's Island, or East Boston, as it is now called, very much resembles a great polar bear, with its head north and its feet east. Governor's Island has much the form of a ham, and Castle Island looks like a shoulder of pork, both with their shanks at the south. Apple Island was, probably, so named on account of its shape ; and Snake Island may be likened to a kidney ; Deer Island is very like a whale facing Point Shirley ;

(134)

THE HARBOR STEAMBOATS AT ROWE S WHARF—Atlantic Avenue, foot of Broad Street.

Thompson's Island, like a very young unfledged chicken; Spectacle Island, like a pair of spectacles; Long Island, like a high-top military boot; Rainsford's Island, like a mink; Moon Island, like a leg of venison; Gallop's (not Galloupe's), like a leg of mutton; Lovell's, like a dried salt fish; George's, like a fortress, as it is; Peddock's, like a young sea monster; and Half Moon, like the new or the old moon, as you view it from the south or the north. The other small islands resemble pumpkins, grapes, and nuts, as much as anything; hence the names of them."

Two defunct forts slumber in Boston Harbor — *Fort Independence*, on Castle Island, and *Fort Winthrop*, on Governor's Island. A third, *Fort Warren*, alive and armed with several hundred watchful eyes, stands guard at the entrance to the harbor, on George's Island.

The Islands.

Castle Island was the first fortified island in the country. Here, in 1634, the Colonists erected rude fortifications, which were replaced, in 1701, by Castle William, a brick fort. This was burned by the British when they evacuated Boston in March, 1776. The Provincial forces then took possession of the island and repaired the fort. In 1797, its name was formally changed to Fort Independence, President John Adams attending the ceremonies. The island was ceded to the General Government in 1798. This island was the scene of many fatal duels in the early days, and a memorial stone of such an event is still standing, which relates that "near this spot, on the 25th of Dec., 1817, fell Lieut. Robert F. Massie, aged 21," and bears these lines:

> " Here Honor comes, a Pilgrim gray,
> To deck the turf, that wraps his clay.'

From 1785 to 1805, it was the place of confinement of prisoners sentenced to hard labor, provision that this privilege should be retained having been made in the act of cession to the Federal Government. The present fort was built about the year 1855, and a small portion of the wall of the old castle remains in the rear part of the fortification. Castle Island, as we have seen in Chapter III, is now a part of the public park system, connected with the Marine Park on South Boston Point.

Governor's Island, just north of Castle Island, was granted to Governor Winthrop in 1632, and was, subsequently, confirmed to his heirs. in 1640 the condition was made that its owner should pay one bushel of apples to the general court, and one to the Governor, every winter. The island continued in the sole possession of the Winthrop family until 1808, when part of it was sold to the Government, for the purpose of erecting a fort, which was named Fort Warren. This name was subsequently changed to Fort Winthrop, in honor of the Governor and the early owners of the island. The uncompleted fortifications on this island may sleep on forever, for modern warfare, with its far-reaching bolts, must be waged many miles from this old stronghold.

Thompson's Island, to the south of Castle Island, has belonged to the city since 1834.

Long Island is about five miles from the city. It contains 182 acres, and has belonged to the city since 1885. Here are a United States lighthouse and a battery. The city almshouse for female paupers, which has accommodations for 500 inmates, is on the island, and other public institutions are to be erected in time. The lighthouse, which was built in 1819, is an iron tower 35 feet in height, and stands on the highest bluff in the harbor. The fixed light is 80 feet above the level of the sea, and can be seen, in a clear night, about fifteen miles. The lantern has nine burners.

Nix's Mate.—East of Long Island Head is a low, rocky island, on which stands a solid structure of stone, 12 feet in height and 40 feet square. All the stones in this piece of masonry are securely fastened together with copper. Upon it rests an octagonal pyramid of wood, 20 feet high and painted black. It is supposed that this monument was erected in the earlier years of the present century, though the date is not known. Its purpose was to warn vessels of the dangerous shoals in the harbor. Why the island is called Nix's Mate is uncertain. There is a tradition that the mate of a vessel, of which one Captain Nix was master, was executed upon the island for killing the latter. But it was known as " Nix's Island " as long ago as 1636, before any execution for murder or piracy had taken place in the Colony, and this would seem to unsettle this theory. It is a part of the tradition that Nix's mate protested his innocence, and prophesied that the island would be washed away. If such a prophecy was made, it has been fulfilled, for the records show that, in 1636, it contained in the neighborhood of twelve acres. There is now not more than one acre of shoal, and there is not a vestige of soil remaining. Several pirates have since been hanged there.

Deer Island, north of Long Island, is where the Houses of Industry and Reformation, the city correctional institutions, are located. The island contains 182 acres. *Deer Island Beacon,* the little lighthouse off the southern extremity of Deer Island, is the newest light in the harbor, having been established in 1890. It is a conical frame tower, in which is a fixed white light, varied by a red flash every thirty seconds. It is visible twelve nautical miles.

George's Island, on which *Fort Warren* is built, lies amid the currents of the harbor, and commands the main ship channel, Nantucket Roads, and the approach to the harbor. Occupied by the only United States garrison in Massachusetts, it is, undoubtedly, the most interesting spot in the harbor. It has not the Puritan traditions of Castle and Governor's islands, for in those early days it was thought too far away to be of much interest. The island was claimed as the property of James Pemberton of Hull, as early as 1622. His possession of it was confirmed, and it was bought, sold, and inherited by various parties until 1825, when it became the property of the city of Boston. It is now, of course, under the jurisdiction of the United States Government. Earthworks were erected on the eastern side of the island, in 1778, for the protection of the French fleet, commanded by Count d' Estaing, then lying in the roadstead, against the attack of British cruisers. In 1833 work on the present formidable fortress was begun, and it was completed in 1850. The granite fortress, designed by General Thayer of Braintree, is built in the shape of a five-pointed star, each point being a bastion. Close to the walls is a deep ditch, the main work being surrounded by a moat, beyond which are other works. The six-acre inclosure is entered through a postern gate, an arch of about five feet in height, opening into another arched portal. When the Civil War broke out there were no guns mounted at Fort Warren and no garrison. Governor Andrew, however, sent the Second Battalion of Massachusetts to the island, cannon were placed in position, and the deserted fortress became a strong defense.

During the war Fort Warren was used as a place of confinement for noted Confederate prisoners. One empty apartment is pointed out as the residence of Mason and Slidell, the Confederate commissioners to Great Britain and France, who were taken from a British vessel bound from Havana to England, and brought here for safe-keeping. They were well treated and enjoyed life in spite of their confinement.

On the morning of January 1, 1862, the emissaries were escorted, with their secretaries, to the wharf and took passage to Provincetown, where they embarked in a British war-vessel and proceeded to England. Alexander Stevens, vice-president of the Confederate States, was also under guard here for five months, in 1865. Generals Gault and Hanson, and Harry Gilmour ; Major-General Johnson, captured, with his whole division, at Spottsylvania, were also among the distinguished prisoners.

Since the Civil War, Fort Warren has not slept. The guns bristle on her battlements to warn off the foreign invader ; up and down strides the ever-watchful sentinel ; inside the walls the men are being trained in the tactics of modern warfare. The only guns that are fired are those to welcome his excellency, the Governor of the Commonwealth, when he visits the post, and at the sunset hour, when their booming resounds across the waters to the neighboring shores.

The fortifications are undergoing changes, to meet the requirements of present methods of warfare, and on the northern and eastern sides of Fort Warren, those sides that look out on the broad sweep of the Atlantic, works of solid concrete are being built that will, when finished and manned with 12-inch guns, make a defense that will practically intercept the entrance of foreign warships to the harbor. These parapets are to be covered with earth, which, when sodded, will present a beautiful and innocent exterior, conveying no hint of the smoldering volcano within. In time, the walls of the southern and western sides will be leveled, to make way for the newer system.

Fort Warren is reached by the trim little steamer Resolute, which runs between Boston and the island.

Lovell's Island, lying to the north of George's Island, belongs to the United States, and is a Government buoy station. It contains seventy-one acres.

Gallop's Island, to the southwest of Lovell's Island, has belonged to the city since 1860. The main ship channel lies between Lovell's and Gallop's islands.

Other islands belonging to the city are: **Rainsford's Island,** containing seventeen acres, on which is located one of the city institutions ; **Spectacle Island,** containing sixty-one acres ; **Apple Island,** containing nine acres, and **Moon Island,** containing about thirty acres, which was taken, by right of eminent domain, in 1879, and constitutes the point of discharge of the great sewer.

Boston Light is about two miles east of Fort Warren, at the entrance of the harbor. **Brewster's Island,** on which it stands, has been a lighthouse station since 1715, when the general court of the Colony ordered one established. During the Revolution the lighthouse was several times destroyed and rebuilt. In 1783, it was once more restored by the State, being built this time of stone, and it has since been enlarged and improved. It is a second-class revolving white light, visible sixteen miles at sea. The tower rises 100 feet above the level of the sea, and can be seen at a great distance, even by day. A heavy fog-horn is also placed here to warn approaching vessels in the foggy weather, which often prevails.

Bug Light is upon the end of a long, sandy spit stretching out from **Great Brewster Island.** It is supported above high water on a system of iron rods fixed in the rocky ledge, affording no surface for the waves to batter and destroy. It is a fixed red light, standing about thirty feet above the level of the sea. It is visible for about seven nautical miles, and is intended to warn navigators of Harding's Ledge, which is about two miles out at sea, east of Point Allerton, and is one of the chief dangers of the harbor.

Seaside Resorts.

Boston is grandly situated with reference to summer resorts. Along the rocky coast of Massachusetts, stretching away from Boston, to the north and the south, in wonderful curves and indentations, including several good harbors, stands a succession of towns where comfort-seeking Bostonians may dwell during the warm months, and yet be within an hour's sail or ride from their places of business. *The North Shore* and *The South Shore,* as they have come to be called, are the natural divisions of this chapter, which present themselves for consideration.

The North Shore.

By the North Shore is meant the northern coast of what was formerly called Massachusetts Bay, but which, on modern maps, is a part of the Atlantic Ocean. It extends from Nahant and Swampscott, on the southwest, to Gloucester and Cape Ann, on the northeast. For the sake of convenience, however, we shall include under this heading several resorts which lie between Boston and Nahant.

Winthrop is a beautiful peninsula, with about eight miles of beach. Summer cottages and boarding-houses abound, and many of Boston's busy toilers find here a refuge for their families during the heated term, which is within easy distance of their places of business. It is reached by the Winthrop branch of the Revere Beach & Lynn Railway.

Hotels.—*Argyle Hotel*—$2.
New Winthrop Hotel—$2.
Shirley House—$1.50.

Revere Beach is a gently sloping beach of sand, several miles long, lying between Winthrop and Nahant, and terminating at the north in *Point of Pines*. Sea-bathing is safe and pleasant in the light surf. There are numerous large and small hotels here, where fish dinners, or dinners of any sort, may be obtained, and thousands of Bostonians come hither on every hot summer day to enjoy the invigorating sea breezes and the sight of the broad expanse of the ocean. At the Point of Pines are fine hotels, and society is somewhat less heterogeneous than elsewhere on the beach. The Boston, Revere Beach & Lynn Railway runs directly along the edge of the beach, affording passengers charming sea views all along the route.

Hotels.—*Gleason House*—$2 to $3.
Russel House—$2 to $4.
Straithmore Hotel—$2 to $4.

Nahant, the oldest watering place on the North Shore, is a rocky promontory, stretching out into the 'sea, nearly at right angles with the coast from Lynn, to which it is joined by a narrow line of sand beach, three miles long, traversed by a single road. It has, for many years, been a favorite resort for old Boston families, and its popularity has never waned among those who have once acquired an interest in its territory. The invigorating coolness of the atmosphere, even on the hottest days; the boldness and picturesqueness of rock effects, and the illusion of being at sea, are among the characteristics which never lose their charm. Along the water's edge, on the eastern side, stands a magnificent array of cliffs, which, for ruggedness and bold beauty, are not surpassed by any on the North Shore. Here is the well-known Pulpit Rock, so named from its shape, to the top of which, in former days, a venturesome young woman climbed, only to discover that she had to be lowered by ropes. The old hotel, which was burned more than thirty years ago, has never been rebuilt. A successful club, organized within the last few years, is the social center which tempts cottagers from their comfortable piazzas. Dwellers at Nahant are distant, by either sea or land, only an hour from the city. Those who sleep at Nahant can enjoy a delicious sail to the city by steamboat, which is, for those who love water, preferable to a heated, dusty railway journey.

At **Bass Point**, the southwestern point of the peninsula which constitutes Nahant, is a comfortable restaurant, where well-cooked meals may be obtained.

Hotels.— *Hotel Tudor* — $3 to $5.
Hotel Nahant — $2.50 to $3.

Lynn is a city of 50,000 inhabitants, on a plain between the sea and a line of rugged porphyritic hills. It is the chief shoemaking place in the world, and employs in that industry more than 12,000 persons. The once well-known Ocean Street of Lynn should not be omitted from any itinerary of the North Shore. It is a short, straight avenue along the sea front. Twenty-five years ago it was divided into fifteen or twenty beautiful estates, of from one to three acres in extent, ranged side by side in stately dignity. They fronted on the avenue, and backed on the full expanse of that portion of the sea which lies under the lee of Nahant. Under the influence of the demand for summer residences, these fine estates have been cut up into smaller building lots, and traversed by connecting streets. The old-time mansions have been pulled down, and, while in a few cases they have been superseded by very elaborate structures, the majority of the new cottages are of the every-day Queen Anne type. Ocean Street is largely occupied by the wealthy shoemakers of Lynn, who live there the year round.

Hotels.—*Anderson House* — $2.
Hotel Oxford — $2.
Prescott House — Special rates.

Swampscott is connected with Lynn by a single shore road, which runs out of Ocean Street. It has, for many years, been a favorite camping-ground of Boston people who wish to live by the sea with as little expense and trouble as possible, and, at the same time, be close to the city. Here are several large hotels and boarding-houses, and many sea-shore villas, with picturesque rocky points and intervening sandy beaches. Many fine water views are obtained from the cottages and hotels.

> Hotels.— *Hotel Preston* — $3.50 to $4.
> *Lincoln House* — $3 to $4.
> *Ocean House* — $3 to $4.

Marblehead.— This quaint old maritime town, in ancient times famous for its fishermen and privateers, is now the center of a group of summer resorts. Marblehead was detached from Salem and incorporated as an independent town, known as Marble Harbor, on May 2, 1649. It is, therefore, one of the oldest towns in New England. It is an interesting town historically and topographically, and its crooked streets and quaint, irregular houses are a study in themselves.

Among the historic houses in Marblehead may be mentioned the large white house, nearly opposite the North Church, where Elbridge Gerry, a signer of the Declaration of Independence, Governor of Massachusetts, and Vice-President of the United States, was born. Col. William R. Lee, of Revolutionary fame, once lived in a house just north of the Common. The hero, James Mugford, who captured the British powder ship, once lived in the house on the corner of Back and Mugford streets. The Lee house, now occupied by two banks, was built by Col. Jeremiah Lee, in 1776, at a cost of $50,000. In its day, it was a princely mansion, and is worth a visit now, for its great halls, its grand staircase, and its carved wainscoting may still be seen. The home of Flood (Floyd) Ireson was on Washington, near the head of Franklin Street. The house is still standing. The oldest building in Marblehead is the old town house, which stands near the junction of Washington and State streets. It was built in 1727, and its walls have resounded to the eloquence of a Gerry, a Story, the Lees, the Ormes, and many others.

On high ground rises Abbot Hall, the most important public building of the present day. It was built, in 1877, from a fund left by Benjamin Abbot, a lifelong resident of the town. A magnificent view is obtained from the tall tower of this building.

Marblehead Neck, which lies just across the harbor, is a peninsula one and one-fourth miles in length and about half a mile in width. It is approached by a narrow isthmus, formed of rocks and sand washed up by the waves. The ocean side is a bluff, rock-bound shore. The harbor, on the northwest side, is nearly a half-mile wide, and is one of the best yacht harbors on the coast. This fact led the members of the *Eastern Yacht Club* to make this their head-quarters, and they built a club-house here in 1880. The *Corinthian Yacht Club* has also a fine club-house on the Neck. Just outside this snug harbor, where the yachts of to-day contend for silver cups, the Chesapeake and the Shannon fired deadly broadsides at each other in the summer of 1813.

The Neck is lined with beach cottages and hotels, and it is second to no sea-shore resort in the country for picturesqueness of surround-ings.

Hotels.— *Crowninshield Hotel* (Clifton)—Special.
Follet House (Marblehead Neck)—Special.
Nanepashemet Hotel—$3 to $6.

Salem Willows.—The tongue of land stretching out and forming the northern boundary of Salem Harbor is known as the Willows. This is a great point of attraction during the summer season, and every provision is made for the entertainment of the crowds who visit it.

Beverly is situated on an indenture of the coast, formed by the harbors of Marblehead and Salem. It was originally a part of ancient Naumkeag, but was incorporated as an independent town in 1668. The fishing business, once quite extensive, is now insignifi-cant, and Beverly is an important shoe-manufacturing town. It is at, and beyond, Beverly that the true grandeur of the North Shore begins. From here to the northeast, as far as the eye can see, lies a marvelous coast, with curving beaches, wooded points, and rugged cliffs, from which you may look out over the blue sea and inhale its fragrance, and, by turning about, find yourself face to face with a rural landscape of quiet woods and green meadows. A succession of fine estates follows the shore, and, almost invariably, the houses stand in the midst of several acres of park-like grounds.

Between Beverly and Gloucester are **Pride's Crossing** and **Bev-erly Farms,** beyond which lies **West Manchester, Manchester,** and **Magnolia,** by which names, for the sake of municipal or railway con-venience, one strip of shore is distinguished from another.

13

Beverly Hotels.—*Hotel Crafts*—Special.
  Trafton House—$2.

Manchester Hotels.—*Masconomo*—$4 to $5.
  Shade Mansion—Special.

Magnolia Hotels.—*Hesperus Hotel*—$3.
  Oak Grove Hotel—$2.50.
  The Magnolia—$3.50 to $6.
  Willow Cottage—$2.

Gloucester is *thirty-one* miles from Boston, by the Boston &
Maine Railway. It was settled in 1633, and it has always been the
important fishing town of this part of the world. Gloucester is in
close connection, by electric cars, with Eastern Point, Bay View,
Lanesville, and other neighborhoods.

Eastern Point.—A large number of hotels and cottages will be
found on Eastern Point, which forms the easterly boundary of
Gloucester Harbor. On the ocean side are the delightful summer
resorts known as *Bass Rocks*, and *Good Harbor Beach*.

Hotels.—*Bass Rock House*—$3.
  Pavilion Hotel—$3.
  The Beachcroff—Special.

The South Shore.

The South Shore of Massachusetts Bay presents fewer striking
contrasts than the North Shore, but it abounds in charming scenery
of sea and land, and it is more emphatically given over to the worship
of the summer boarder. From Downer Landing and Hingham,
around the queer little peninsula, on whose extremity stands the
town of Hull, to Plymouth, the shore is lined with boarding-houses,
hotels, and summer cottages.

Downer Landing overlooks the broad southern expanses of the
harbor, and it is one of the most delightful resorts near the city. It
is reached by steamboats, which run from Rowe's Wharf eight or ten
times daily to Hull, Nantasket, Downer Landing, and Hingham.
Twenty years ago it was Crow Point, the home of a few cows, that
roamed at will over its breezy hillsides. It is a place of quiet, picturesque views, and here one may bathe in water that is less cold and
more shallow than at the other beaches. Among the attractions of
Downer Landing may be mentioned the Melville Garden, with an
area of twenty acres, wherein are offered various amusements—boat-

ing, fishing, bathing, dancing, bowling, shooting, and opportunties for playing billiards, ball, croquet, tennis, lacrosse, and other games. Swings, flying-horses, and all sorts of sport are provided for children. It is a great resort for picnic parties from all sections of Eastern Massachusetts. One of its features consists of an immense clam-bake pavilion — seating nearly 1,000 people at one time — where mammoth heaps of clams are baked upon stones, upon which a hot fire has been burning, placing over them seaweed to hold the heat. Ears of green corn are cooked in the same manner and at the same time. These clam-bakes are greatly enjoyed by the crowds who flock to Downer Landing on hot summer days, crowding the harbor steamers to the limit permitted by law.

Hotel.—*Rose Standish House*—$3.

Hingham.— After calling at Downer Landing, the steamer proceeds up the tortuous harbor of Hingham to the quaint old town, which stands at its head. Hingham has many pleasant drives, with fine views of sea and harbor. The visitor will be charmed with the old Colonial houses, and " The Old Ship," the oldest church edifice in the country, dating from 1681, and still in use. In the adjacent graveyard are the statue and tomb of John A. Andrew, the War Governor of Massachusetts, and the monument of General Lincoln, of Revolutionary fame. Hingham is on the New York, New Haven & Hartford Railway, which connects with the railroad running north to Nantasket Beach and Hull.

Hotels.— *Lincoln House*—$3.
        Cushing House—$2.

Hull is a quiet little town, of less than a thousand inhabitants, standing at the end of the peninsula, which stretches north from the South Shore, and forms a natural breakwater, which protects Boston Harbor. Here, on the high hill, which commands a view of the entire harbor, is the observatory, from which the arrival of vessels, their names, and the point from which they sailed, are telegraphed to the Chamber of Commerce in the city. Hull is only a half-hour from Boston by steamer, and it is the terminus of the railroad, a branch of the New York, New Haven & Hartford Railway, which runs the entire length of Nantasket Beach, a distance of five miles.

The leading hostelry of the place is the Hotel Pemberton — $4.

Nantasket Beach is to Boston what Coney Island is to New York, in point of accessibility, and the various attractions and amusements provided for visitors. But in its picturesqueness and natural beauty, in the reasonableness of its hotels, and in the character of the crowds who throng it on warm summer days, it is far superior to the monotonous sand beach which is the delight of the metropolis. It is one of the most beautiful beaches in the world, sweeping round in a majestic curve, almost as even as a floor, miles in length, and offering unrivaled facilities for bathing, walking, driving, and lounging. There are aquariums, merry-go-rounds, miniature elevated railways, skating-rinks, Punch-and-Judy shows, and all the amusements which are provided to tempt the dimes from the pockets of good-natured visitors. Then there are the fakirs, with toy balloons, whips, peanuts, pop-corn, and lemonade, helping to swell the excitement and clamor; and dime museums, where circus acrobats and fat women pose for the entertainment of those who find pleasure in such shows. This beach is lined with hotels and restaurants, which cater to the day excursionists, most of whom scarcely leave the immediate vicinity until they take the steamer for the return trip to the city. No one should leave Nantasket without having taken the drive over the Jerusalem Road, one of the most famous roads in the country, along which one sees a succession of beautiful summer homes.

Hotels.— *Atlantic House* — $3 to $4.50.
   Black Rock House — $2 to $3.
   Kermohassett House — $2 to $3.
   Nantasket House — $2.
   Rockland House — $4.

Nantasket is reached by steamer from Rowe's Wharf, eight or ten times daily, and by the Old Colony division of the New York, New Haven & Hartford Railway to Hingham, thence by the Nantasket Beach Railway.

Cohasset is twenty miles from Boston by the New York, New Haven & Hartford Railway. It may be reached from Nantasket by carriage drive over the beautiful Jerusalem Road, above alluded to. It has a noble, rocky sea front, and is one of the most picturesque and romantic spots along the South Shore. A large theatrical colony have their summer homes here. Off shore is the famous Minot's

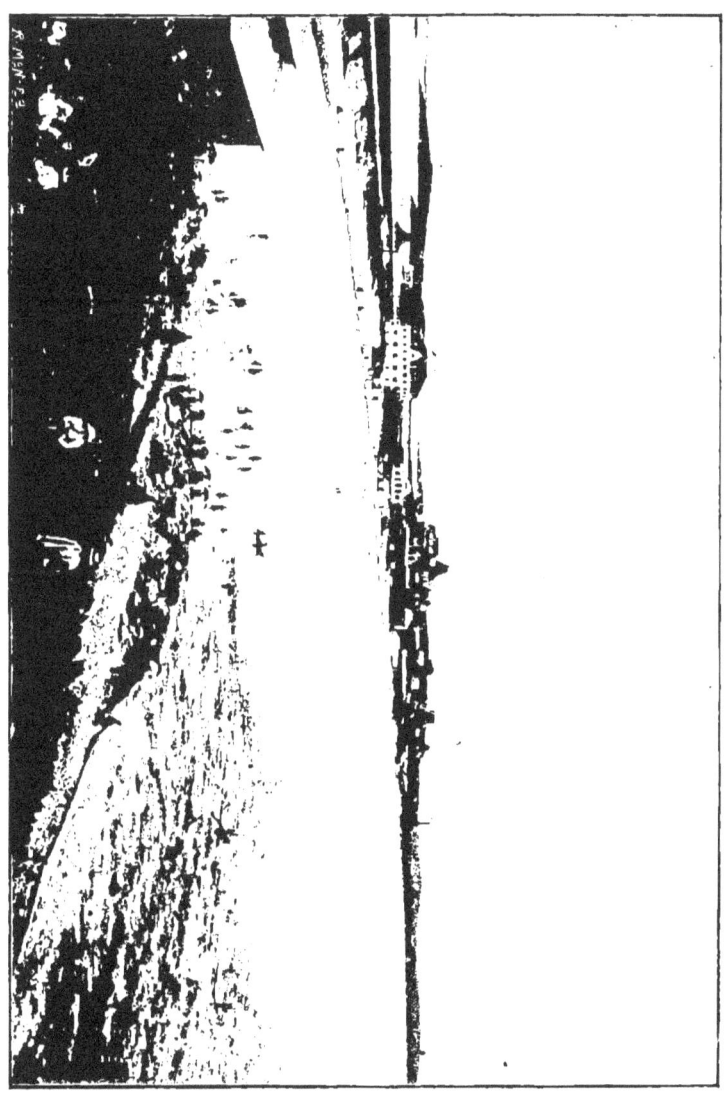

NANTASKET BEACH.

Are You Reading

The New Traveler?

8 to 16 Pages

One Cent

"Boston's Best
Evening Newspaper."

Light, a tall tower of masonry, rising from out the ocean and warning navigators of the treacherous Cohasset rocks.

Hotels.— *Beals House* — Special rates.
Black Rock House — $3.
Cohasset Hotel — $2.

Scituate is a little town of less than 3,000 inhabitants, on the New York, New Haven & Hartford Railway. Like other places along the shore, it has picturesque bluffs and beaches, with pleasing views over the bay and across the little harbor of the port. Near **South Scituate** is the estate of a Mr. Worthy, the original of the "Old Oaken Bucket" house. Samuel Wordsworth, the poet, lived here with his stepfather, Mr. Worthy, great-grandfather of the present owner. In 1817 he wrote the well-known poem, and the well still gives forth cold and sparkling water.

Hotels.— *Coleman Heights Hotel* — $2.
Mitchell House — $1.50.

Marshfield, the home of Daniel Webster, is a quiet seaside place where fishing, yachting, and shooting can be enjoyed to-day as well as when the great statesman here found relief from public cares and worries. Of him everything speaks. Hotels bear his name or boast that he once made them his resting-place; and of these, possibly, the best known is the *Brant Rock House*, where, in the fall, hundreds of wild fowl may be shot from the very windows. The hotel is directly on the beach, within a few feet of the high-tide line, and in front of it lies the famous rock.

Hotels.— *Brant Rock House*—$2.
Fair View House—$2.
Humerock House—$3.

Duxbury is a picturesque and delightful old Puritan town, where the *Anglo-American Cable Company* has its station. This was originally the *French Atlantic Telegraph Company*. Near the summer resort of **South Duxbury** rises the sightly *Captain's Hill*, crowned by a lofty round stone tower, erected as a memorial of Miles Standish, the military leader of the Pilgrim Colony, who lived at the base of the hill. This was also the home of John Alden, the hero of Longfellow's beautiful poem; Elder William Brewster, and other historical worthies.

Hotels.— *Hollis Hotel*—$2.50.
Powder Point House—Special rates.
Standish House—$2.50.

Plymouth, the resting-place of the Pilgrims, is often called the Mecca of the United States. It is a quiet little town of 8,000 inhabitants, with charming views across its broad and shallow harbor and out over the broad Atlantic. Back of it are leagues of lake-strewn forest, " The Adirondacks of Massachusetts," where herds of deer still linger. Plymouth would be a most desirable summer resort if there were no historic associations to supplement her superb natural attractions. As it is, however, the first-named qualifications are those, mainly, that are widely known, and thousands of visitors to her scenes yearly discover that in her woods and shores, her hills, roads, and magnificent rural situations, and in her glorious blending of land and ocean scenery, to say nothing of the salubrity of her climate, she is entitled to claim recognition as one of the finest watering-places in the country. For the benefit of those persons who think only of " Plymouth Rock," the " Mayflower," and other historic matters, when visiting this famed town, the following information is presented: The idea of building a monument to the memory of the Pilgrim Fathers was early entertained in Plymouth, and became the definite object of the Pilgrim Society upon its organization, and, through the efforts of this society, the National Monument to the Pilgrims was erected in 1889. The monument grounds are on Cushman Street, and from them fine views of the harbor, bay, and roadsteads are to be had ; of the " Cowyard," where the " Mayflower" lay at anchor ; of Clark's Island, upon which the Pilgrims passed their first Sunday ; of the Miles Standish Monument, surmounting Captain's Hill, in Duxbury, and of much fine scenery, if the weather be favorable.

The total height of the monument is 81 feet from the ground to the top of the head of the statue. Following are some of the dimensions or this work, said to be the largest and finest piece of granite statuary in the world : Height of the base, 45 feet ; height of statue, 36 feet. The outstretched arm measures, from shoulder to elbow, 10 feet 1½ inches ; from elbow to tip of finger, 9 feet 9 inches ; total length of arm, 19 feet 10½ inches. The head measures around at the forehead 13 feet 7 inches. The points of the star in the wreath around the head are just 1 foot across. The arm, just below the short sleeve, measures 6 feet 10 inches around ; below the elbow, 6 feet 2 inches. The wrist is 4 feet around. The length of the finger pointing upward is 2 feet 1 inch, and is 1 foot 8½ inches around. The thumb measures 1 foot 8½ inches around. The circumference of the neck is 9 feet 2 inches, and the nose is 1 foot 4 inches long. From center to center of the eyes is 1 foot 6 inches. The figure is 216 times life-size.

The plan of the principal pedestal is octagonal, with four small and four large faces. From the small faces project four buttresses, or wing pedestals. On the main pedestal stands the figure of Faith, one foot resting upon Forefathers' Rock, the left hand holding a Bible; the right, uplifted, pointing to heaven. On each of the four smaller, or wing, pedestals is a seated figure. They are emblematic of the principles upon which the Pilgrims proposed to found their Commonwealth. The first is Morality, holding the Decalogue in her left and the scroll of Revelation in her right hand. Her look is upward toward the impersonation of the Spirit of Religion above. In a niche, on one side of her throne, is a prophet, and in the other one of the Evangelists. The second of these figures is Law : on one side Justice, on the other Mercy. The third is Education : on one side Wisdom, ripe with years ; on the other Youth, led by Experience. The fourth figure is Freedom : on one side Peace rests under its protection , on the other Tyranny is overthrown by its powers. Upon the faces of these projecting pedestals are alto-reliefs, representing scenes from the history of the Pilgrims — the Departure from Delft Haven, the Signing of the Social Compact, the Landing at Plymouth, and the First Treaty with the Indians.

Returning from the monument grounds to Court Street (the main street), and passing the head of Old Colony Park, the first interesting point of visitation is Pilgrim Hall, on the same side of the street with the park, and distant from it about thirty or forty rods. Within this hall will be found a museum of Pilgrim memorials and curiosities.

A short distance from Pilgrim Hall, still keeping upon Court Street, the court house occupies a commanding site on the right, a pretty lawn in front. In this building are to be found many valuable and curious documents, including the Patent Documents and Records of the Colony, the will of Miles Standish, etc. These will be shown upon application to the Registry of Deeds.

The court house is situated at the base of Burial Hill, on the north; but, to visit this famous spot, it is better to return to Court Street and continue the walk southward. At the head of

North Street, the name of the main thoroughfare changes from Court to Main Street, and the course is directly through the business section of the town. Main Street soon abuts upon Leyden Street, the first street laid out by the Pilgrims, and abounding in their memorials to this day. Arrived at Leyden Street, on the right, looking westward, is Town Square, and beyond the square the gravestones of Burial Hill are in full view.

On the left, or eastward, the street runs directly to the water front, a side street at the brow of the hill, opposite the *first house*, winding northerly to Cole's Hill, which overlooks the Rock and its canopy.

From Burial Hill a series of the finest outlooks imaginable are afforded, including scenes and localities of greater or less historic importance; and all the immediate neighborhoods are centers of historic associations. Here is the site of the ancient fort, which served as a meeting-house, and toward which the Pilgrims wended their way with muskets upon shoulder or swords in place. The graves of Pilgrims are in every part of this elevated burying ground. Looking outward over the ocean waters, the course of the "Mayflower," her anchorage, Clark's Island, the Gurnet, and all the harbor and bay situations connected with Pilgrim adventures are in full view. Landward some notable localities of Council Fires and Indian Feasts are to be seen. From Burial Hill standpoints the town lies literally under one's feet.

Main Street has three streets abutting upon and running at right angles with it — North Street, Middle Street, and Leyden Street ; and each of these leads directly to Cole's Hill and the water front, overlooking the Rock and the shore line. Cole's Hill was the place of burial of many of the Pilgrims who died during the first winter, their graves having been carefully concealed, so that the Indians might not know of them. Here were buried, also, many Indians. The Rock and the original Landing Place are at the base of this steep hill, and a few steps brings the visitor from its brow to the canopy over the Rock. In the War of the Revolution, and in that which followed from 1812 to 1815, fortifications were maintained upon this hill.

As the distances oceanward are somewhat deceptive to unpracticed eyes, it may be here noted that from the water front opposite the canopy of the Rock, the distance to Gurnet Light is within a small fraction of five miles. The length of Plymouth Beach, which forms the outer protection of the harbor, from the Manomet Hills to the extreme point of the beach, is a little more than three and a half miles. The beach, from head to point, is two and five-eighths miles in length. When the Pilgrims landed, this beach was largely covered with forest growth, in which deer and other animals common to the Plymouth woods to this day roamed.

A ride on the electric railroad, which pursues the line of the water from Kingston Village to Hotel Pilgrim, near the base of the Manomet Hills, will make available a constant succession of harbor and bay views, from constantly changing standpoints, and is one of the best experiences possible to the visitor to the Plymouth locality. If this ride is supplemented by a drive to some more inland point or points within a short distance of the shores, the delights of the Plymouth trip will be indefinitely multiplied. A visit in this way to Morton Park, one of the finest provisions of its kind; Billington Sea, South Ponds, or the White Horse neighborhoods, or in almost any direction along or away from the water front, will richly repay the trouble and expense in making it, and afford the visitor an appreciation of the natural beauties and resources of this ancient town.

The *Plymouth Steamboat* makes one round trip daily from Sargent's Wharf, passing the forts and islands mentioned elsewhere in this chapter. Outside of Boston Light, it turns to the southward, down the Old Colony Coast, passing Nantasket Beach, Minot's Ledge Lighthouse, Cohasset, Scituate, Marshfield, and Duxbury.

Plymouth is also reached by the Old Colony division of the New York, New Haven & Hartford Railway.

Hotels.—*Hotel Pilgrim—*$2.50 to $3.
  Manomet House—$2.
  Samoset House—$2.50 to $3.

INDEX.

(152)

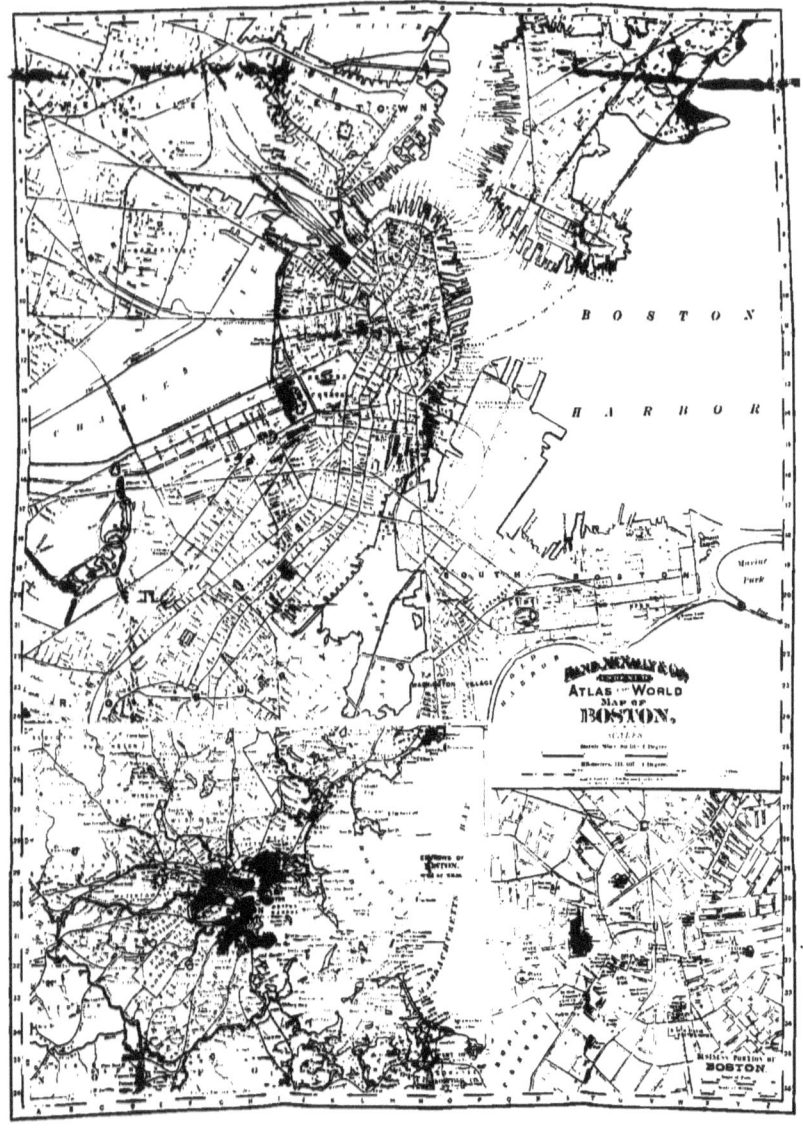

RAND McNALLY & CO.

ATLAS OF THE WORLD
MAP OF
BOSTON,
SCALES

BOSTON HARBOR

ARMSTRONG'S

Railway Dining

.. AND ..

News Rooms

ᴜoston & Albany Railroad

and branches. Passenger Station, Boston, and other points on line of road.

ᴏston & Maine Railroad,

Northern, Southern, Eastern, and Western, and all other Divisions. New Union Station, Boston, and others on that road.

ᴵitchburg Railroad

and its branches. New Union Station, Boston, and other places on that road.

ᴵncord & Montreal Railroad

and branches. Passenger Station, Manchester and Concord, N. H., and others on line of road.

Boston, Revere Beach & Lynn Railroad.

Passenger Station, Boston, and other points on road.

Central Passenger Station. Taunton, Mass., Old Colony System of
N. Y., N. H. & H. R. R.

GEORGE W. ARMSTRONG.

General Office, 80 Utica St. (Opposite Boston & Albany Passenger Station).

BOSTON, MASS.

Leaks in Business.

The little losses make the difference between success and failure in business. Thousands of New England merchants have turned these little losses into gains by the use of a National Cash Register. We would like to talk the matter over with you personally. A postal card will let us know you are interested.

HIGH & HOYT,
No. 177 Washington Street, BOSTON, MASS.

Mellish, Byfield & Co.

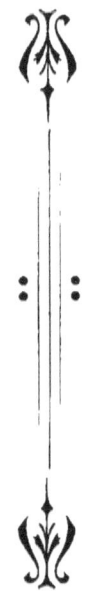

MERRILL & CO.,

Wholesale Commission
Merchants in ⸺

FRUITS _{AND} PRODUCE

11 North Market and 11 Clinton Streets,

BOSTON.

☞BANANAS a Specialty.☜

Boston Potato Chip and
Vienna Pop Corn Works

Boston Potato Chip Co., Proprietors.	OFFICE AND MANUFACTORY, 139 BLACKSTONE ST.

Grocers, Provision Dealers, Bakers, and Lunch Counters
furnished with Fresh Chips daily.

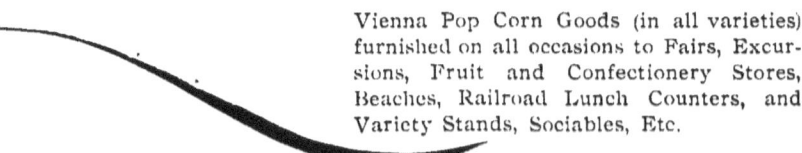

Vienna Pop Corn Goods (in all varieties)
furnished on all occasions to Fairs, Excur-
sions, Fruit and Confectionery Stores,
Beaches, Railroad Lunch Counters, and
Variety Stands, Sociables, Etc.

Goods manufactured in various flavors
and fine in quality.

Your Orders Solicited.

A. W. MITCHELL MFG. CO.

Badges—
Door Plates..

Dog Collars, Seals, Stencils,
  Burning Brands, Baggage Checks,
    Steel, Brass, and Rubber Stamps.

..CHAS. J. LITTLE..

200 Washington Street,   —BOSTON, MASS.

POOL BROTHERS

WHOLESALE DEALERS IN

BEEF, PORK, LARD, HAMS
FLOUR
TRIPE, TONGUES, DRIED BEEF, PIGS' FEET,
BEANS, ETC.

Boston Agents for the Springfield Provision Co.

NO. 20 SOUTH MARKET STREET,

W F. POOL.
J. V. POOL.   ————BOSTON.

Batchelder Bros.

COAL AND
WOOD

No. 356 Federal St.
Telephone, 1156. . . . . .

Boston.

Fabulous Sales of Popular Novels.

G. W. Dillingham, Publisher, New York, seems to have the art of making novels go in times good or bad. During an interview with Mr. Dillingham, a few days since, he was asked to what he attributed his great success. He replied: *"Study, work,* and *judicious advertising,* but the greatest of these is *advertising."* He said that he had sold the following numbers of the books of his most popular authors ; the figures are certainly *immense :* Mary J. Holmes, nearly 2,000,000; May Agnes Fleming. 750,000; Augusta J. Evans, 400,000; Albert Ross, nearly 1,000,000; Marion Harland, 500,000; J. Esten Cooke, 85,000; Mayne Reid, 170,000; Julie P. Smith, 120,000; New York Weekly Series, 200,-000; A. S. Roe, 125,000; Frank Lee Benedict, 80,000; Allan Pinkerton, 175,000; Chas. Dickens, 450,000; M. T. Walworth, 90,000; Celia E. Gardner, 80,000; M. M. Pomeroy, 60,000; Victor Hugo, 110,000; Ruffini, 15,000; and of books other than novels : Artemus Ward, 20,000; Laus Veneris, 13,000; Michelet, 100,000; Renan, 30,000. The above is only a partial list of the books with large sales issued by Mr. Dillingham.—*New York Tribune.*

M. J. CONANT & CO.

. . . DEALERS IN . . .

Butter, Cheese, and Eggs

21 AND 22 SOUTH MARKET STREET.
27 CHATHAM STREET

M. J. CONANT.
W. S. VINCENT.

BOSTON.

NEWTON A. HOAK. ESTABLISHED 1845. JAMES MISOCHI.

CHAS·KIMBALL·&·C⁰⁻

WHOLESALE AND JOBBERS

Foreign and Domestic

ORANGES,
LEMONS,
BANANAS,
APPLES,
CRANBERRIES, Etc.

Fruits and Produce

Potatoes,
Sweet Potatoes, Onions, and Eggs...

Cor. Atlantic Ave. and Clinton St.
BOSTON

TELEPHONE CONNECTION.

FINEST GROWN.

Albert E. Hughes

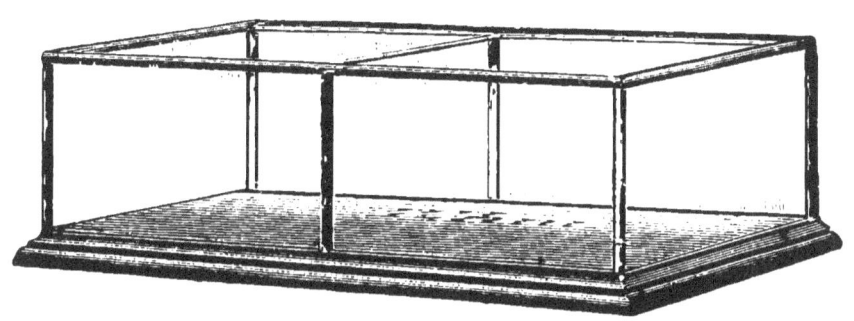

SHOW CASES

309 WASHINGTON STREET,

OPPOSITE OLD SOUTH CHURCH,

BOSTON.

EASTERN
FISH
CO<u>MPANY</u>

WHOLESALE AND
RETAIL DEALERS IN

Fish
❖ Lobsters
Oysters
&c.

180 Eliot Street and 34 Carver Street

BOSTON

E. B. WADSWORTH, Proprietor

Why Pay High Prices
For Imported Cigars ?

The Corina
Cigars——

Are the same stock, at less price,
made by Spanish workmen. . .

FOR SALE AT ALL STATIONS ON THE

Boston & Maine, and
Boston & Albany Railroad,

. . . BY . . .

GEO. W. ARMSTRONG.

The Rival
——Bouquet

Is Sold at the Depot Stands and on all the Trains.

. . . .

Its Fine Aromatic Flavor Pleases Everyone.

. . . .

DON'T FAIL TO TRY

THE RIVAL BOUQUET

. . . .

FOR SALE BY

GEO. W. ARMSTRONG.

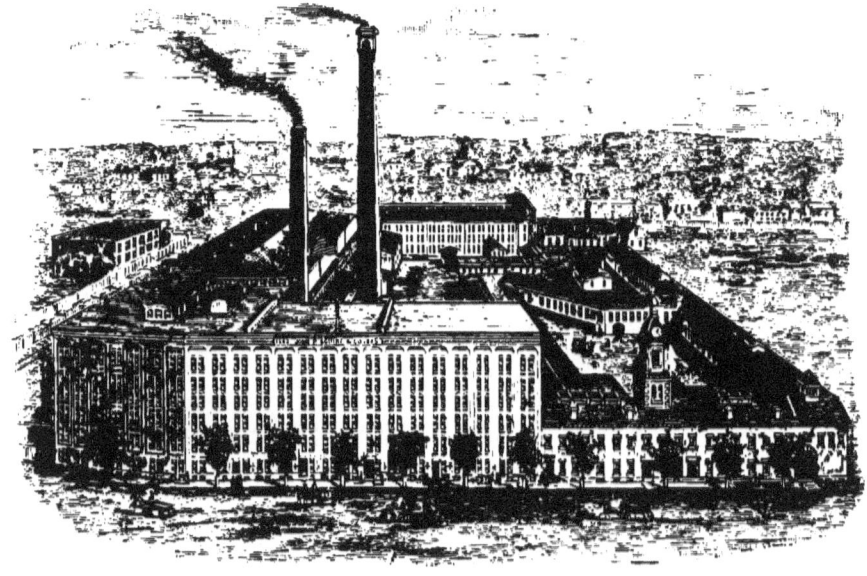

We Advocate

Compulsory education of the children of
immigrants in our public schools.

The improvement and protection of the
public school.

The restriction of immigration of all classes,
and the prohibition of immigration of all
unworthy and vicious.

The total prohibition of the use of public
funds for sectarian purposes.

The removal of sex discrimination in suf-
frage, and the restriction of the ballot to
the intelligent and worthy.

The taxation of church property.

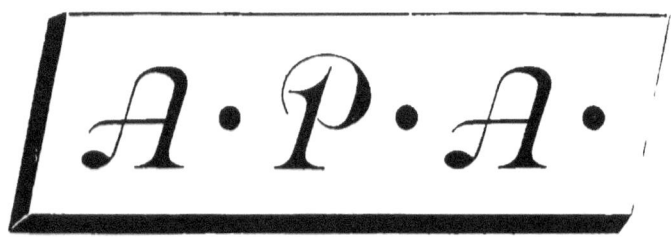

For eight years we have advocated these
principles, during which time our con-
stituency has grown from fifteen hundred
to tens of thousands.

THE AMERICAN CITIZEN

7 Broomfield Court, BOSTON.

ALL NEWSDEALERS, - - FIVE CENTS.